BROTHER OUTLAW

Brant Avery rides into the little town of Gunsight, seeking revenge for the death of his brother Greg, accused of rustling and lynched five months previously by a gang of Circle C riders. Almost immediately, he is confronted by Sheriff Tex Euston, who warns him not to go shooting off his piece. Brant is determined to clear his brother's name and see justice done — if not by bullets, then by the law. But the lynchers are out on bail, and prosecutor Jared Larrabee refuses to present a case against them without witnesses or evidence. It's up to Brant and Tex to find out what Circle C beef was doing in Greg's corrals, speak to those who saw the crime and persuade them to testify, and confront Don Yoder — foreman of the Circle C, and the man who set the noose . . .

SPECIAL MESSAGE TO READERS

THE ULVERSCROFT FOUNDATION
(registered UK charity number 264873)
was established in 1972 to provide funds for
research, diagnosis and treatment of eye diseases.
Examples of major projects funded by
the Ulverscroft Foundation are:-

- The Children's Eye Unit at Moorfields Eye Hospital, London
- The Ulverscroft Children's Eye Unit at Great Ormond Street Hospital for Sick Children
- Funding research into eye diseases and treatment at the Department of Ophthalmology, University of Leicester
- The Ulverscroft Vision Research Group, Institute of Child Health
- Twin operating theatres at the Western Ophthalmic Hospital, London
- The Chair of Ophthalmology at the Royal Australian College of Ophthalmologists

You can help further the work of the Foundation
by making a donation or leaving a legacy.
Every contribution is gratefully received. If you
would like to help support the Foundation or
require further information, please contact:

THE ULVERSCROFT FOUNDATION
The Green, Bradgate Road, Anstey
Leicester LE7 7FU, England
Tel: (0116) 236 4325

website: www.foundation.ulverscroft.com

BROTHER OUTLAW

LEE E. WELLS

SAGEBRUSH
Large Print Westerns

First published in Great Britain by Curley
First published in the United States by Ace Books

First Isis Edition
published 2018
by arrangement with
Golden West Literary Agency

A catalogue record for this book is available
from the British Library.

ISBN 978–1–78541–547–0 (pb)

Published by
F. A. Thorpe (Publishing)
Anstey, Leicestershire

Set by Words & Graphics Ltd.
Anstey, Leicestershire
Printed and bound in Great Britain by
T. J. International Ltd., Padstow, Cornwall

This book is printed on acid-free paper

CHAPTER
ONE

Had the storm come out of the Canadian wilds a month ago, it would have piled snowdrifts against every building of Gunsight, and would have blocked all the roads with white barriers. But this late in the year it poured rain and Gunsight's main street ran with runnels of steel-gray water. It drummed on the roof of the sheriff's office and dripped with dismal insistence from the eaves, so that Tex Euston nodded sleepily to the sound and shivered inwardly.

He arose from his desk and glanced at the stove. Heat radiated pleasantly into the room and Euston sighed comfortably as he pushed blunt fingers through iron gray hair and walked to the front window.

Gunsight, to his limited view, was a miserable huddle of rain-drenched buildings. The street was a quagmire turning into a minor river. No one moved along the street and there was not a horse tethered at any of the long hitching racks. Tex sighed, relieved, and wryly wondered if peace depended on bad weather.

Euston made a wry grimace, his wide, liver-colored lips moving under the sweep of white mustache that made strange contrast with his darkly sallow skin. He suddenly wanted to forget the office and the meaning of the badge he wore, take this rain-soaked time of peace for a drink, a pleasant chat with almost anyone. He recalled that he needed some rifle shells, and the thought salved his conscience.

The Cattle Bar was on the way to the hardware store and, by the time Tex had been buffeted by the gusts of wind, the saloon loomed as a welcome haven. He turned off the mud-smeared plank sidewalk and climbed the few steps to the porch. Rain drummed constantly on the roof just above his head. He took off his hat and shook the water from it, grinning at the dark sky, then turned to the beckoning warmth of the saloon.

The moment he stepped inside he realized that there would be a slight flaw in the smooth, pleasant flow of his thoughts. Three men stood at the bar, boot heels hooked on the dull, brass rail. The tallest of the three men glanced carelessly over his shoulder, then turned full around, resting his elbows on the polished wood behind him.

"Well! the law of Gunsight!"

Euston hid the irritated twitch of his mouth by stroking his mustache. The other two were Circle C riders, men he had long since tagged as little more than animated echoes of their *segundo*.

"A bad day to be riding, Yoder," he said to the man who hailed him. "What brings you to Gunsight?"

Yoder thumbed his hat back from a high, dark forehead. The overhead lamp cast deep shadows along the high ridge of his arrogant nose, touched the prideful, wide lips, the harsh eyes. His sheepskin coat

2

was open and the brass shells in his gunbelt held a dull glitter.

"Why, Tex, not long ago you wanted mighty bad to keep me here! Ain't changed your mind?"

Euston took the glass the bartender placed before him and downed the whiskey with a quick toss. The short chuckles of Yoder's two companions irritated him more than Yoder's open taunt. "No, Don, I ain't changed my mind. Someday you'll have room and board at my place."

"Now, Sheriff, you're saying the judge was wrong about us?"

Euston looked away. His pleasant mood was shattered but he hoped to save a bit of it. He put a coin on the bar, pulled his coat up around his neck. Yoder watched him obliquely. Euston started toward the door, stopped short, turned. Yoder still watched him.

"I've lived a lot of years, Don, and have seen a lot of ranges and towns."

"So?" Yoder asked carelessly.

"So, I've learned one sure thing. A man rides too high and mighty, he gets throwed sooner or later."

Yoder grinned. "Now what could you mean by that, Sheriff?"

"Something for you to chew on, Don. I've never yet met a man or a combine of 'em too big for the Law. The Association ain't no bigger than some I've seen."

Yoder's head went back and his laughter was loud, grating. "But big enough for Gunsight, Sheriff. Plenty big for that."

"But something always comes along," Euston said dourly and walked to the door, and out into the rain-swept street.

He turned into the general store. The pleasantly sharp and oily smell of hardware struck him and the lights dispelled the gray gloom of the rain. He moved down an aisle and the pungent smell of a barrel of apples made him take one and munch as he continued back to the gun rack. Brittmeyer waited on two customers, a man about Euston's age and a young woman. They looked around and the man nodded curtly.

"Howdy, Tex."

Ed Dahl held a rifle and Euston thought that this could mean more trouble. Then he called himself a fool for always seeing trouble. That's what came of wearing the badge too long — or ramroding law in Gunsight the last three years. He nodded to Dahl.

"Surprised to see you in town on a day like this, Ed And you, Miss Helen."

The girl smiled, her sea-green eyes lighting in genuine pleasure. She was not tall, but a slender, curved body gave that impression. She wore a sheeplined coat, a dark skirt of a fine cloth. Her voice had a slight throaty quality

"A ranch runs out of supplies, Tex, no matter the weather."

Euston nodded and Brittmeyer said, "Be with you in a minute."

"I can help myself — shells."

4

He selected two boxes from the shelf, held them up and Brittmeyer nodded that he would charge them. Euston looked sharply at the rifle in Ed Dahl's hands.

"Getting varmints out on Spade?" he asked.

"Not lately," Dahl said. "Thought I'd do a little hunting before spring round-up."

"Stay clear of the hills," Euston said dryly, "or someone might hunt you. Wouldn't like to write to your Eastern bosses that they lost a ranch manager."

Dahl grinned but said nothing. Helen wandered down the aisle and stood near the door, examining a bolt of cloth, then bending to eye beads in a showcase. Euston walked toward the door and Helen looked up as he approached. Tex wished they'd made girls that pretty when he was young. Might've married one of 'em instead of carrying a law badge over half the damn' country.

"Don Yoder's in town," he said. "I could figure on seeing you if Don's around."

She blushed and the heightened color increased her beauty. "It doesn't necessarily follow," she said lightly.

"A bad day," he grunted, "for the worst dog alive. A man would be a fool to venture far from a warm stove."

"A fool?" Helen asked and laughed. "Then there goes one."

A horse and rider slowly rode down the street. Mud streaked them both and the man's heavy coat had absorbed water for hours. His hat was dark stained with it and drops fell from the wide, curled brim. He was hunched against the wind.

5

Helen and Tex Euston watched him with mild curiosity. Tex noted the wide spread of the shoulders, the lithe sway of the body to each step of the horse. He could not clearly see the face, just an angle of the long jaw, the planed cheek. The man came closer then plodded by. He was directly before the window now but he did not see the sheriff and the girl. His head lifted just then and he looked about. Both Tex and the girl gasped.

They had seen a ghost . . . that of a man who had kicked out his life at the end of a rope some five months before. Circle C riders had strung him up on a tree limb in a narrow canyon and it was said that Don Yoder himself had set the noose. But Greg Avery's dead! Tex fiercely told himself.

He looked at Helen. She stood, wide-eyed and staring. Some of the color had left her face. She stared at Tex, unbelieving, frightened for the moment, questioning. Tex moistened his lips.

"Got to get along," he said.

"That man," Helen said in a low whisper. "It couldn't be . . . Greg Avery?"

"Course not!" Tex snorted. "Some chuckline johnny riding through — happened to look a little like him in this poor light." He laughed. "Sure gave me a start, though."

"And me." Helen's full lips pursed and she glanced out the window again. The rider had ridden beyond sight. She laughed, dismissing the incident. "Funny how you can fool yourself."

6

"It sure is." Tex hurried by the saloon, stopped at his office just long enough to open the door, place the cartridge cartons on the floor and hurry on. He glanced back down the street to the hotel and the livery stable, across the river of thick mud that now passed as a street. Euston saw no one in the wide, black maw of the livery stable, nor was Lashbrook at his usual spot before the dusty office window.

Euston splashed across the mucky ruts of the street. Mud sucked at his boots but at last he reached the hotel. He did not check to scrape the mud from his boots on the crescent-shaped iron blade set before the door, but strode into the lobby. His eyes cut to the row of three cracked leather chairs ranged beside the dusty rubber plant. None of them was occupied. The clerk, a balding man in black vest and shirt sleeves, looked up from a solitaire game spread on the desk. He saw the mud on Euston's boots and his thin lips set in prim disapproval.

"Tex, even if you wear the badge . . ."

"Forget it, Lathe. More important business." He glanced toward the door. "Pay no attention to me, savvy?"

"But, what . . ."

Euston saw the shadow of the man across the front doors. He made a warning gesture to Lathrop Stevens and dropped into one of the leather chairs. A second later the door opened. The stranger stopped just within, closed the door behind him and leaned against it as though the weight of a long and grueling trail pressed hard upon him. Then he pulled off his hat, the water showering upon the faded carpet. Lathrop's dry, prim voice broke the silence.

"Would you do that in your own home, mister?"

"Reckon I might," the stranger answered. His voice was just this side of basso and held the ghost of a drawl. Now Euston could see him squarely. Greg Avery — with changes, the same — yet different.

He had the same long, lean face with the jutting chin, rock hard for all the cleft just below the wide, irregular lips. The cheeks were high-planed and the skin was dark. His hair was thick and black and he could use a barber. This man had Greg Avery's black brackets of eyebrows, the long nose with the slight hump in the ridge.

His eyes were light; Euston couldn't yet tell their color. The stranger opened his coat and now Euston noted the worn holster, the plain-handled Colt nestled in it. The man's shoulders were wide, square and his chest was deep. For all his weariness, he walked to the desk with a smooth stride that hinted at flowing muscles in those long legs, the tapering back.

"A room?"

"We have vacancies," Lathrop answered.

"Kind of like a front one," the stranger said. "I always watch people walk by."

"Particular, ain't you?"

The man laughed, a deep sound that held little mirth. "Sometimes, yes. Again, no. This time I am."

"We've got one. Sign the register."

The man accepted the pen Lathrop pulled from the potato, dipped into the inkwell and extended to him. As

8

he bent over the register, Euston arose and reached the desk in three long strides. His own coat was open now and the badge glittered on his shirt pocket. The stranger straightened, then realized someone stood close.

He turned, lazily. Now Euston saw that he had gray eyes with something of the color of the lowering rain clouds. They were set well apart with little crinkles in their corners, caused by either wind or sun, or maybe laughter.

Lathrop turned the register around and he made a gurgling sound. "Brant Avery!"

The man's black brows made twin, questioning peaks and a light smoldered far back in the gray eyes. His glance had touched on the badge, the gun, and then rested full on Euston. He waited, nothing more. He might go for his gun, he might wheel about and run, he might argue, or laugh or . . . he might continue to wait. There was no way of knowing from the unmoving face.

"Greg's brother," Brant said evenly.

Tex sucked in his cheeks. "Intend to even the tally?"

"You're Tex Euston?" Brant asked in return, "the man who wrote me about him?"

"I'm Euston, sheriff of Gunsight and the county about."

"You didn't say how he was killed, Sheriff . . . just that he was. You didn't say who did it, or why. Didn't you think I might be curious?"

"He's dead — five months. Didn't you wait a hell of a long time to work up your curiosity?"

"Sheriff, I was on a trail drive and your letter waited until I got back to the home ranch. I got curious the minute I read it. How . . . why? . . . and who?"

"The ones who hung him said they caught him with stolen beef." Euston stiffened when he saw the flash of anger in the calm eyes.

Avery breathed deeply. "You doing anything about it?"

"All I can. The lynchers surrendered themselves to the judge. He set bail and released them, pending trial."

"When's the trial?"

"Soon's the prosecutor can build up a case that'll hold." Euston's white brows knotted down. "That don't satisfy you, does it?"

"If it was your brother, would you be satisfied?" Brant asked.

"So you plan to handle things yourself, Avery?"

Brant nodded. "That's right. You aim to stop me?"

It was a direct challenge, given in a low, quiet voice. Euston's jaw set and a muscle jumped in his cheek. His hand slashed down to his gun but Avery's blurred and the barrel of a Colt touched Euston's stomach just above his gun belt. He stood frozen, his gun not quite clear of the holster. His eyes bugged and Lathrop gasped, hands flat on the desk, jaw hanging open.

Tex Euston took a deep breath and he looked down at the Colt. He did not flinch. Behind the counter Lathrop stood still and quite pale. Brant waited, letting the silence pile up, gray eyes calm. Tex looked up at him and contempt showed in the curve of his lips.

"Gunslinger. I reckon I could've expected it." He glanced down at the Colt again. "How long you figure to hold the upper hand?"

"Long enough," Brant replied.

"To do some killing," Euston snapped. "Gunsight will be mighty unhealthy, Avery. I don't know what you got in mind but . . ."

"You intend to stop me?" Grant demanded.

Euston didn't hesitated. "Yes . . . if you plan to ride a manhunt trail. You've planned to take the law into your own hands, kill your own skunks. I won't let you."

"You talk big," Brant said gently and there was, strangely, neither sarcasm nor boasting in his tone. His eyes softened and tension left the harsh, lean face.

"I wear a badge," Euston said evenly. "I keep the law."

Brant's face lighted and he suddenly balanced the gun a moment and then with a swift, smooth motion dropped it back in the holster. He grinned and turned to Lathrop.

"How about a room — pronto?"

Lathrop caught himself. "Oh . . . Oh, sure!"

Brant Avery again faced Euston. "I've read your sign wrong, Sheriff. I apologize."

Euston blinked, not quite believing this. "I could run you out of town, Avery, for shoving a gun in my ribs."

"You could," Brant nodded soberly and then the grin flashed again, this time with an edge. "But I'd come back." He picked up the key Lathrop eagerly dropped on the counter.

"No point in us growling around, Sheriff. Come up to my room. We've got a lot to talk about."

CHAPTER TWO

Brant waited and Euston stood indecisive, still irritated by the way the man had immediately dominated this first meeting. Lathrop eyed first Brant and then the sheriff, and his avid curiosity became a sharp prick of annoyance.

"We'll talk," Euston said at last. "But it'll change nothing."

"Sure."

Brant led the way and Euston was forced to follow. Just as Brant reached the stairs there was a scurrying sound from the counter and he turned to see Lathrop hurriedly shrugging into his coat.

Brant chuckled. "He's going to tell the town. He can't wait to spread the news. Nothing we can do about it."

Euston started to snap an angry order at Lathe, then the truth of Brant's statement hit him. With a grunt, he turned to follow Brant up the stairs and down the narrow hall to the front of the building.

Brant found his room, inserted the key and opened the door. The room was surprisingly large and a single big window, runnelled with rain, overlooked the street. The bed was of heavy carved wood with a thin mattress covered by a sheet and a gray blanket.

"Well, I reckon this is home for a while. Mighty mean weather you have up this way, Sheriff."

Euston stirred impatiently as Brant unbuckled his gun belt and hung it from the back of another chair. "What you aim to do about your brother?"

"When you wrote that letter, what did you think I'd do?" Brant doused his face in the water and scrubbed.

Euston waited until he reached for the towel. "I don't know what I expected . . . but more sense than this. You've come up here to notch your gun."

"You're talking," Brant said noncommittally and briskly scrubbed his face.

Euston walked to the window, glanced carelessly on the muddy street. He wheeled about and his voice lifted. "Avery, I've done all I can to bring those lynchers to trial. But I'm tied hand and foot."

"What's tied you?" Brant lifted his head and his eyes were cold as twin gun muzzles.

Euston made a helpless gesture. "Our prosecutor says that without witnesses we couldn't prove a thing but hearsay, and we sure as hell couldn't convict 'em."

Brant picked up his shirt. "You can't move and the law can't move. So no one pays for Greg. Well, maybe I can."

Brant donned his shirt and stood, arms hanging loose, lean face dark and ugly, searching Euston for some further clue to the lawman. He had the dark, lithe grace of an Indian.

Brant's lips hardly moved and his voice was low. "My brother was hung. The killers can't be brought to trial. You don't want me around. How's a man to figure

14

that?" His voice dropped. "Maybe you take orders or pay from someone. Maybe that's why you won't . . ."

Euston's fingers taloned into Brant's shirt front. The lawman's leathery face twisted in anger and his white mustache quivered. "I was never bought in my life, Avery. I've never been scared out of doing my job. I ought to kick your teeth down your throat for that."

He shoved Brant away and the man caught himself against the wall. He smiled and there was no anger in him for what the lawman had done. Euston lifted a long, gnarled finger and shook it under Brant's nose.

"Don't ever speak that idea again. You know better."

Brant's smile vanished as he nodded. "I apologize, Sheriff. I figured a place that'd let a man be hung without a chance to defend himself would have no idea of a fair deal, for me or anyone else."

Euston made a harsh grimace and shook his head "That's been true in some ways, Avery. Right now, I can't do much about it. Nor I won't let you . . ."

"I'm not a gunslinger," Brant cut in. "I don't intend to notch any guns unless it's forced on me." He sat down on the bed and gestured the sheriff to take the chair. "But something could be done, and I figure I can help — one way or another."

"How?" Euston demanded.

"How can I tell yet?" Brant asked sharply. "I thought I'd find out what happened, see what the Gunsight country is like. Then I'd try to work with the law to make sure Greg is cleared of a rustler brand and his killers are brought to taw — legal."

"Then . . . downstairs?" Euston asked.

"You were set for trouble and hoping it would come along. You wore a badge, but a star has hidden a gunslinger time and again."

Euston stroked his mustache, looked at the window, judged the time and then nodded. "Let's go see Jared Larrabee. He's the prosecutor. You can get the whole story and find out where we stand."

Brant lifted the gunbelt from the chair, strapped it about his waist. He put on his coat and scooped his hat from the floor. "Lead the way."

The rain had slackened when they stepped out on the hotel porch, but the street still ran water and the earth was a gummy, black porridge. Euston indicated Gunsight's single brick building on the main corner. Lamps in Gunsight's bank cut the gloom of the lower rooms while above lamps lit a few offices.

Both men set their collars about their necks rugged at their hats and stepped off the porch. They reached the far side, their boots mud caked, and Euston led the way to the entrance just back of the bank. Narrow, carpeted stairs ascended to an upper hall and gloomy shadows lurked in the corners.

A step sounded, there was a rustle and Euston drew back as a woman came down the stairs. She hesitated and then came on. Brant and Euston pressed against the wall to let her by and the dull light touched a tall and slender figure in an enveloping dark coat. Brant had a brief glimpse of an olive face with enormous brown eyes, velvet soft.

Euston spoke in pleased surprise. "Why, Miss Lois! I . . ."

"Have you seen my father, Tex?" she asked. Her voice was clear, musical, but hurried with slight excitement. Her glance went to Brant and then swung away.

Euston shook his head in regret. "Maybe at the store. Miss Lois."

"Yes, at the store!" she echoed and gave the lawman a nervous smile. "I'll look there. Thank you, Tex."

She swept down the last step or two and out the door. Euston put his hat back on his head and turned to the stairs again. He looked back at Brant. "That was Lois Carter."

Brant nodded, not too interested. Euston added. "She's Ray Carter's daughter. He owns Circle C." His tone implied that this should be of significance.

A narrow hall led to the front of the building. Brant followed Euston about halfway down the hall where the sheriff opened a door and entered a small room, reception to a larger one beyond. The far door opened and a tall young man, face eager and alight, came out. He looked blank for a second, then saw Brant and the color drained from his face. He caught himself and a veil dropped over his eyes, changing their blue to something cold and hard.

"This is Jared Larrabee," Euston said. "And this is Greg Avery's brother. He's come to learn about Greg, so I brought him here."

"Of course," Larrabee said but Brant sensed this was not at all to his liking.

They moved into the inner office and Larrabee seated himself before a big rolltop desk. He looked to be about thirty. He might shade Brant by an inch, but his body lacked Brant's solid build. His skin was fair, the head proudly set on his shoulders. His mouth was wide, the lips full and mobile, set pleasantly until Brant noticed the faint arrogance in their corners.

His hair was corn-gold, waving back from a high forehead. The blue eyes were veiled now, but they could be as cold and cruel as Spanish spurs. Larrabee was dressed in the conservative long black coat and vest of the lawyer, and his shirt was creamy white, broken by a short, dark blue tie. A small ruby glinted from a gold ring on his right hand.

"Jared, there's a lot about the Greg business that Avery don't understand. Some of 'em beat me, too, being honest about it. I reckon you can tell him as well or better'n anyone."

Larrabee nodded. He was at ease now, a touch wary but sure of himself. He looked directly at Brant. "What can I tell you?"

"All of it," Brant said shortly. "I just got a letter and a few facts, a whole corral full of ideas that might be right or wrong."

"I can understand," Larrabee nodded. He had the full, flexible voice of the orator. He swung the swivel chair half around so he could look out the window. The rain still runnelled across it and, as the day waned the light lessened.

"Greg Avery ran a store, saloon and corrals out on the Smoky Hills Road. It's not far from the broken country and Greg was too friendly with the men who wandered down out of the breaks and canyons."

"Implying he was one of them?" Brant said, clipped.

18

Larrabee impatiently shook his head. "Implying nothing. Want to hear the truth or just the part that fits your own ideas?"

Brant frowned and then shrugged. "All of it."

"Greg built up a good business out there, mostly from the little ranchers up in the draws. He liked 'em and he talked for 'em against the Association every chance he had."

"This Association?" Brant asked.

"The big outfits in this part of the country are banded together," Larrabee replied patiently. "They pool market news, breeding and ranching methods. They police themselves. Most of the ranches are owned by stockholders in the east, or in England or Scotland. The Association acts as clearing house. It sets up policies . . ."

"It goes into politics," Euston said in a growl. "It owns the territorial legislature. It passes laws and those it can't, it enforces anyhow with a little gunsmoke."

"Or hanging?" Brant asked swiftly.

Larrabee cleared his throat. "I won't go that far, but you get the idea of the Association. Greg dealt in cattle, buying a few head, selling them. Some said he wasn't careful where he bought nor did he look at the brands too closely." He lifted his hand as Brant started to protest. "In any case Don Yoder, foreman of the Circle C, and four of his riders found Circle C beef in his corrals. It was a special gather Carter had ordered. They were stolen."

"Greg never stole anything," Brant said.

"Yoder claimed they were stolen and his riders supported him. Greg Avery was never a man who could hold his temper. Don Yoder's not noted for patience, either. So Circle C handed out the usual range justice to a rustler. They hung him."

Brant tried to calm the ragged rhythm of his breath. "Justice? Did Greg have a chance to explain how Circle C beef got into his corral?"

Larrabee sighed. "I used the word loosely, Avery. I don't know if Greg had a chance or not. Yoder and the others never made that clear. Lee Hinson, a homesteader up that way, came into Gunsight and told Tex he'd found Greg."

"He said he'd seen the hanging at first," Euston cut in. "Then he hedged on that and we can't be certain of anything except he found Greg."

Brant leaned forward. "You arrested this Yoder and his riders?"

Larrabee cut in. "We didn't have to. They came into Gunsight and surrendered to Judge Kilbain."

"Then why," Brant fell back in the chair, "aren't they in jail?"

"Judge Kilbain set bail . . ." Larrabee started.

"Bail! For murder!" Brant almost shouted.

"I am not Judge Kilbain," Larrabee said. "He must have found some precedent in law for it. In any case, he set the bail high enough, five thousand dollars each. The bail was posted and they were released pending trial."

"Twenty-five thousand dollars," Brant said. "This Association posted it?"

Larrabee glanced at Euston. "As a matter of fact, no. They posted bail for one another."

Brant looked blankly at him, then at Euston. The sheriff made a grimace. "Judge Kilbain allowed them to post bond for one another, over their own signatures and marks."

"A foreman — and four punchers!" Brant said, amazed.

Euston grunted. "They couldn't raise five hundred a man, let alone five thousand!"

Brant looked steadily at him and slowly the anger mounted, sending a dull red color in his lean cheeks, cording his neck. "What in the hell kind of justice is this!"

"Association justice," Larrabee said flatly. He stirred, looked at Brant with wry pity. "It's a brand of justice you get used to in Gunsight. Men have bucked it for a time . . . your brother did . . ."

"Now wait," Euston cut in. "You don't believe half of that, Jared. We were elected by the little boys, the townsfolk and homesteaders. Association tried to beat us but didn't get anywhere, except Judge Kilbain."

"Yes," Larrabee agreed. "But sometimes I think . . ." He broke off. "Back to your brother, Avery. Under the circumstances, we can't arrest Yoder or put him in jail. All we can do, is bring him to trial."

"And you've waited five months?" Brant demanded.

"We'll wait longer." Larrabee dropped his steepled hands, blue eyes piercing and hard. "Get the facts in your head, Avery. You only try a man once for murder. What does it take to convict?"

"The truth," Brant said. "The facts."

Larrabee eased back in his chair. "And how do we get 'em? Lee Hinson denies now that he saw the hanging. Jim Wolf worked for Greg when it happened and so did a boy named Kit Thomas. Jim Wolf has disappeared. Kit Thomas is now on Spade, an Association ranch, and can't be reached. There might be one other witness . . . Belle Rainey. She — stayed out there. But she's gone. If I bring a man to trial, I want a conviction. If there's not enough to present a case, I don't present it."

"You'll let it die!" Brant accused.

Larrabee impatiently shook his head. "I wait for evidence for witnesses. Then I'll make a case all right."

Brant's eyes met and locked with his. At last Brant pulled himself up. The window was almost dark but Brant strode to it and looked down on the rain-wavering lights from the stores and saloons. His fingers drummed on the ledge. He turned to find both the young attorney and the old sheriff watching him.

Now he had the full story — or was it? He was inclined to trust Tex Euston, sensing behind the man's pepperiness a steel purpose and strong principle. Jared Larrabee? Brant was inclined to like him on first sight, and yet there were certain subtle things that worried him.

A powerful combine of ranchers, against them a determined group of small cattlemen who had wrested the mechanism of the law from the more powerful by the sheer number of their votes. Greg had supported them and Greg had been hung out of hand by an Association foreman and his riders.

Was that the whole truth? Had Greg actually run stolen cattle, or was this a means to silence him? Were there hidden personal motives and jealousies involved? Damn it! He had only the top of it, those facts obvious to everyone! He needed more.

His lips pursed and he again looked sharply at the two men. He slowly walked back to his chair and sat down looked at Larrabee, and his cold gray eyes held the man. "Evidence . . . witnesses . . . that's all you need?"

"That's about it, Avery."

"And that's the whole damn' rub," Euston added. "I tried to work on Lee Hinson but got nowhere. He sticks to his story, the way he told it the second time. I've watched for Jim Wolf. He's gone for sure. I reckon Belle's up in the hills with her kin and she can't be found. I've done all I can but there's no witnesses."

"Yoder and the others admit it," Brant said.

Larrabee smiled patiently. "Avery, what cattlemen wouldn't shoot or hang a rustler caught stealing his beef? They'd be released with little more'n a jawing from the judge and a light fine. But there's hard feelings in Gunsight. The people expect me to get more than a fine. But — we're stopped. For all we know, Yoder and the boys will change their stories at the trial. We have nobody who saw a thing — who set the rope, who kicked the horse — if Greg had stolen cows, or if he didn't. What kind of a case is that?"

Brant rubbed his hands together, blindly staring at them. His head swivelled to Euston. "You asked me what I aimed to do, Sheriff. I think it's pretty plain by now. Larrabee, if I find witnesses and bring 'em in to testify, then you'll bring this to trail?"

Larrabee looked startled, then his face cleared and he smiled. His voice was firm. "I will. But — what can you do?"

"I don't know," Brant said and arose.

"Whatever it is, I'll sure as hell help you," Euston said.

"This sounds very fine," Larrabee said slowly, "but I don't think . . ." He cut off short and held out his hand to Brant. "Hell, I'm pessimistic! I wish you luck, Avery. My record would look good with five new convictions. Bring in the evidence."

Brant accepted the hand. Larrabee's clasp was warm and firm, his blue eyes direct and alight now. Brant and Euston walked to the door, Larrabee just behind them.

Brant stepped out in the hall, leaving Euston to follow. He had just reached the head of the stairs when the sheriff joined him. They went down the steps, silent, and then with one accord stopped to bundle their coats against the rain.

Euston spoke dryly. "You don't make friends easy, Avery."

"Depends — when — and who."

"Now a smart man would look around first and then decide who'd make a good friend," Euston said. "Better git to my office."

The rain, the gloom, the chill, the mud, all seemed a part of the horror that had happened to Greg. Brant's lips moved in silent anger, in a dislike for Larrabee who

24

had hinted Greg might have been in league with the rustlers.

Euston abruptly left the walk, climbed a couple of steps and threw open the door of his office. The pot-bellied stove no longer glowed so redly and the shadows had conquered the room. Euston moved through the half-dark with familiar certainty and struck a match. A lamp cast a false warm glow over the room.

Euston opened the stove door, threw wood into its iron maw. Brant found a seat near the desk and watched until the sheriff settled behind his desk, considered Brant judiciously a moment. "Well, now you know the story."

Brant stirred. "What about Jared Larrabee. He's . . . all right?"

Euston laughed, a short and final sound. "Jared Larrabee was born in these parts. Went to law school and come back. He was elected prosecutor by the little ranchers and the townsmen. I reckon that tells you."

"Reckon it does." Brant rubbed his fingers along his upper lip, frowned at the stove. Maybe he was too suspicious, reading signs where none existed. That could easily be, since Brant had met Larrabee but once. He looked directly at Euston.

"You know now what I intend to do. Make me a deputy."

Euston grinned, a tigerish and disbelieving smile. "Nope, not yet. I've heard you talk but I ain't seen you act. I don't take a chance on putting a gunman behind a badge. But if I see you're playing it as you've called it, I might change my mind. Blame me?"

25

"No," Brant conceded. He smiled and his face became suddenly boyish. "I reckon I don't have an honest face. I'll be around for that badge later. Now what can you tell me about Greg?"

Euston knew little more than Larrabee and could give no important new information. When Euston finished Brant wearily arose from the chair.

"Well, it's been a long day and a long ride. I'll see you."

"Tomorrow?" Euston asked.

Brant shrugged. "Maybe a whole bunch of tomorrows."

He closed the door behind him, walked to the edge of the canopied porch and looked back, as though trying to read some significance in the steady glow of yellow lamplight through the dusty windows. At last he walked away, heading for his hotel.

In his own room, he shucked off coat and hat, tried to remove the street's gumbo from his boots. He washed and carefully combed his hair in the wavy mirror over the dresser.

He considered Larrabee and Euston and weighed such new information as he had learned. He had a job, a big one . . . no doubt about it. He picked up his coat, paused, staring at the dark window and the night that pressed against it. Greg slept out there somewhere in the muddy ground. Someone would pay for that. Brant's chin hardened and there was a small jumping muscle in his cheek up near the ear. His lips pressed tight, relaxed, and he picked up his hat, closing the door and locking it after him.

The hotel had no dining room but there was an entrance from the lobby to the cafe next door. Brant followed the scent of cooking and was soon at one of the dozen tables. He ordered from a red-faced and curious waitress, but he gave her no more than a smile.

He ate the first big, hot meal he had tasted in days. With a sigh, he pushed the plate aside, refused a fourth cup of coffee and paid his bill. He arose, feeling pleasantly warm, glad that the dismal night was beyond the walls and the windows. He sauntered into the lobby, started toward the stairs.

A man blocked his way. Brant started around him but another man was beside him. Brant pulled up, alert. He stood in the center of a ring of armed, wary-eyed men. They watched him, tense and yet challenging, as though they expected him to explode into violence. A hard, round object pressed into Brant's back.

He looked over his shoulder into the face of the handsome man he had seen in the cafe. The man's lips peeled back in a smile and Brant saw the cruel dance of lights in his dark eyes. At the same moment, he felt his Colt lifted from the holster.

"Nice night for riding," the man said, "and getting acquainted." He nodded toward the outer door. "Coming along?"

CHAPTER
THREE

Brant's gaze moved slowly around the tight ring of men. The gun in his back was still a hard warning. His lips flattened slightly and then even this slight sign of anger was hidden under the calm mask of his face.

"Looks like you're calling the tune."

"And you're dancing to it, friend."

"Not too sure about that . . . yet."

"I am," the man rapped. He jerked his head toward the door. "Let's look at the moon."

Brant moved at an easy pace to the door. The men pressed close and, as he stepped out into the dark night, Brant had a last glimpse of Lathrop's pale countenance the eyes large for the pasty face. The street was a wedge of the dark broken by pinpoints of light for a little distance before they were swallowed up by the stygian, cosmic curtain.

A voice hailed them from the hitchrack. "Waiting — right here."

The gun muzzle was a steady pressure. Brant descended the steps, circled the hitchrack. The moment he left the wooden planks, mud sucked at his boot heels. The rain had stopped but there were dark clouds scudding close over head. Brant was shoved along the line of horses and then halted His nostrils flared when he realized that someone had brought his own mount from the livery stable, saddled ready to ride. These men did not intend for him to come back.

"Hit the leather, friend," the leaders voice rapped.

Brant took the reins and swung into the saddle. Others had mounted about him and one pressed close. Brant caught the dull glitter of metal in the man's hand. The group swung away from the hitchrack and moved down the street.

The lights of the town wheeled by and then were far behind. Free of the town, the night and the clouds gained a new intensity, a brooding quality as though they waited for this minor human drama to be played out before they again took the center of the stage. They rode for miles. There was no talk, only the creak of leather, the sodden plop of hoofs in the muddy road. Darkness pressed close.

"This is it," the leader said, his voice flat.

They reined in and there was restless movement, a half turn of the horses, a toss of head, a man easing forward in his saddle and back. The leader moved up to Brant, leaned forward on the saddle horn.

"You're Greg Avery's brother." It was both a statement and a question.

"I am," Brant answered.

He caught only the blurring end of the movement in the shadowy figure before the coils of a lariat cut across his face. Only by a cowman's instinct he grabbed the saddlehorn and his legs tightened convulsively. He rocked back into a firm seat and at the same time kicked his horse forward, his hands reaching for the man.

Someone grabbed his horse's cheek strap, another slammed a fist at him and he felt the pressure of gun muzzles in either side. He heard the ominous click as the hammers dogged back. He sat unmoving, holding in his anger, his arms rigid and his jaws ached as they clamped tight. He spoke in a sibilant whisper.

"You're the bunch that murdered Greg."

The leader's raucous laugh held a cruel delight. "Now how in hell did you guess that!" His voice grew sharp. "And it could happen to you, Avery, right here and now. It depends on how much sense you've got."

He waited but Brant did not reply, not trusting his voice. The man pressed close. "I got an idea why you've come here. You've made a mistake. Greg Avery only got what was long coming to him. Everyone knew he was a rustler."

Brant caught his voice. "Did a court know, Yoder, or do you think you're bigger than a court?"

"Well! So you know me!" Yoder's voice held gleeful surprise. "Then maybe you know how we give a man what's coming to him. Law, courts and all that jawing are only a waste of time and money. A thick tree branch and a lariat does the job a hell of a lot quicker."

Brant's anger had made him cold and filled with a bitter sarcasm. "Of course, you boys just did the citizens a favor and no one could blame you!"

"That's right," Yoder said.

30

"Liar!" Brant spat. "Then why did you run hellbent for the protection of a crooked judge! You're killers . . . and you know it. You're scared — everyone of you."

"By God!" Yoder blazed and his hand slashed down to his side. The gun whipped up, but one of the riders cut between Yoder and Brant. Yoder tried to force his horse around him but the man kept blocking his chance of a shot. A dozen voices rose in protest, one above the others.

"Don! Get your feathers down! Ain't we had enough trouble with these damn' Averys already!"

Yoder at last held his horse in, and his breath sounded ragged and gusty. Brant no longer felt the pressure of the guns but their menace had not been removed. His face stung where the lariat had slapped him and anger constricted his chest.

"All right," Yoder said at last. "Well handle this another way."

"Ride him out, Don," one of the men said. "He'll know better'n to come back."

"To make sure, we'll give him a taste of the rope," Yoder snapped. His voice lashed at Brant. "Get off that horse, Avery!"

Brant sat unmoving. One of the men pulled his horse in close. 'Avery! We're running low on patience.'

Brant took a deep breath and deliberately dismounted. He stood in the mud and glared up at the black, looming shapes of the horsemen. They had fallen back so that now he stood within a crude half circle, facing Don Yoder.

Yoder glared and moved slightly. A loop dropped abount Brant and before he could lift a hand it tightened about his body, constricting his arms to his side.

"This is more'n you deserve, Avery," Yoder said. "It ought to be around your neck. But maybe it'll give you an idea of how healthy Gunsight will be for you."

He whipped his horse around and his spurs touched its flanks. It lunged away and the rope tightened. Brant jerked off his feet, went sailing through the air. He could not move his arms to cushion his body or head.

He hit the sea of mud and water. He was pulled and rolled helplessly in the quagmire, half-drowned. Had the ground been dry he would have been seriously injured. As it was he felt as though great sledges pounded at his chest, his ribs. Mud and water was forced into his nose, his eyes, his mouth. Once he felt as though his right ear had been ripped from his head. The rope was a steel ring about his body with a sharp knife edge that cut into his flesh, sawed through his arms. Then his head struck some solid object. Lights flashed and glared in his brain, then snapped out in complete darkness.

Something rocked his head back and forth, strange objects sent sharp slivers of pain through his dulled brain. He became aware of his aching body, of the clammy grip of water and mud. His eyes snapped open. He lay on his back and dark shapes hunched over him. A hand slapped across his face and then backhanded another blow. Brant moved his head and made a moaning sound. The shape straightened and Brant became vaguely aware that a man stood spread-legged above him. A voice came from nowhere.

"He's come around, Don. Thought for a minute you'd killed him."

Another tall and sinister shape joined the first, stood high a moment and then crouched close. Brant thought he recognized the harsh voice — someone he didn't like. His brain stirred and his paralysis snapped. He recognized Yoder, the riders who now stood grouped around him. From somewhere beyond he heard the stir of horses. Yoder's voice brought Brant's attention back to him.

"Avery, you've had a sample. There won't be another. You can sit out here and think it over. Then get on your horse. Ride far, friend, and don't ever come back."

Brant started to pull himself up but Yoder placed his hand against Brant's chest and contemptuously shoved him back into the muck. His voice was flat, yet deadly.

"Just remember what happened to Greg. Next time we see your face, it'll happen to you."

Yoder arose and moved back to the horses, the men following him. Brant raised himself out of the mud and sat there, the dark world spinning. It steadied and he realized that the horses milled as the men swung into the saddle. Once more there was a sudden silence. Yoder's voice came as from a distance.

"Your horse is ground-tied right here. Head out and always keep your back to Gunsight." Suddenly he laughed, the sound brittle and harsh. "Easy riding, friend!"

They wheeled and rode away. The squashy sound of hoofs was loud for a moment, then faded. Brant sat alone, still dizzy, bruised and battered, mud-covered, and the chill of the water penetrating into his bones. The night pressed close about, enwrapped his body in a clammy grip.

At last he half-turned and winced at the sudden pain of a twisted muscle, a bruised rib. He gritted his teeth and tasted dirt between them, but he pulled himself up on his feet and stood swaying, fighting the dizziness. He heard a slight movement just ahead and his vision cleared enough to see the shadow of his horse. He wiped his hand across his mouth and only plastered more mud on that which already masked his face. His clothes pressed against him, wet, heavy with the gumbo. Water and mud had been forced down into his boots and his feet felt encased in a jellylike ice.

He took a breath that clawed painful fingers along his ribs and into his lungs. His hat was gone and his muddy hair pressed like a tight cap against his skull. He took a step, swayed, recovered and then grimly plodded the few yards to his horse. But he had strength only to grab the saddle and hang on, leaning against the animal, gathering strength.

At last he fumbled for the stirrup. He lifted himself up and dropped into the saddle. He held to the horn, swaying. At last he squared his shoulders despite the protest of chest muscles and ribs. He stared into the darkness and half lifted the reins.

He weakly touched his spurs to the horse and the animal turned to the pull of the reins. Gunsight was now at Brant's back. What difference would it make to Greg one way or the other? He was dead, unseeing, unhearing, unfeeling. Brant winced as the horse moved.

Brant shivered, pressed his eyes tightly. He pulled the horse in. Dead! The outlaw brand placed on him never to be erased. Maybe that would matter to Greg. Brant's head slowly lifted. It mattered to Brant! Thief, rustler and outlaw! Greg? Any of the Averys? Brant? The stigma extended to him even as it stained the memory of Greg.

Brant clenched his teeth, set his bruised jaw and shivered against the penetrating claw of the wind. He tightened his grip on the reins and turned the horse about, his feeble kick urging it forward. Now Gunsight was somewhere ahead and each plodding step brought him closer. He swayed several times in the saddle and more than once the urge came to turn about again, be sensible, not risk his life for a man five months dead. Brant fought these thoughts and the nausea and the pain that swept over him.

He became aware of misty pinpoints of light far ahead. He drew rein and stared dully until he realized he looked once more on Gunsight. The town repelled and beckoned, warned and encouraged. The fights glowed steadily, a challenge and a symbol.

Brant edged his horse off the road, intending to make a wide circle and drift into Gunsight from a different direction. Yoder might be waiting for him.

His horse stumbled slightly, caught itself. The jar sent a bolt of pain up his spine, but it cleared his brain.

He passed the back of his muddy hand across his bruised lips and his eyes glinted.

His real job had started, just at this moment.

CHAPTER
FOUR

The gray, yet penetrating light awakened Brant and he looked out through the window onto a sky made of steel. The light hurt his eyes and he closed them, aware now of the luxury of the bed. He felt that if he moved, he would bring back the pain of the night before, the shaking chill of the wind and the mud.

He thought of the painful trip back to town, his wandering in the shadowy back ways until he reached the livery stable. He vaguely remembered the hostler's surprise when the muddy figure slipped off the horse. Brant had warily searched the dark street and slipped into the hotel. The clerk must have been asleep behind the counter for there had been no sign of him when Brant staggered across the lobby, pulled himself up the stairs.

He still had no clear recollection of how he had undressed or had washed off the mud and slime. But now, when he lifted his hand, it was fairly clean. He stirred and his muscles instantly cried a stiff protest. He nevertheless moved his feet out of bed and slowly stood up. He looked at himself in the mirror. His eye was discolored and his lips puffy. He found several dark blue marks on his body and legs and there was a red burn about his chest where the rope had mercilessly cut. He bent painfully to the bowl and scrubbed his face, then attacked his hair, still thick and matted.

He spent a torturous hour removing the traces of last night's muddy encounter, but at last he shrugged into a clean shirt feeling that he might face the world again. He started to strap on his belt and saw the empty holster, the cartridge loops caked with hard, brown mud. His Colt undoubtedly lay somewhere out on the range, buried hock-deep in clogging mud — a good weapon ruined.

His gray eyes flinted. Something else to add to the score. He turned to pick up his hat and his glance swept the street, centered on a couple walking along on the far side. The man was dressed in a black shirt, blue levis and a heavy, short coat. His hat hid his face until he threw back his head and laughed at something the girl had said. Brant instantly knew that handsome face, with the high-bridged nose, the flash of teeth behind the full lips. Don Yoder!

Brant first saw only Yoder's proud, swinging stride. Then he became aware of the girl. She was not tall, and yet her slender body gave that appearance. Her head was set proudly and he glimpsed a swirl of bronze hair escaping from the pert bonnet. Her figure was curvesome and her face beautiful.

Yoder touched her arm in a proud and possessive way. The couple passed out of the range of his vision and Brant caught himself with a start. He had no time to be interested in any girl Yoder might know, when he was concerned only with forcing the man into jail.

The clerk, Lathrop, was again behind the desk when he went downstairs. He glanced at Brant, away, and then his head jerked back and he stared hard, swallowed. "What . . . ?" He caught himself.

Brant's lips moved in a painful quirk. "I fell out of bed, friend. You ought to make your floors of soft pine."

He nodded curtly and strode out the door, leaving the man to stare after him, jaw hanging. The wind that stirred along the muddy street was chill and penetrating. It had stopped raining but the air was damp, saturated with its cold residue.

Brant looked at the hitchracks, saw but few saddled horses. There was no wheeled traffic on the street, probably would be none until the ground dried and folks could come in from the ranges. Brant wondered where Yoder's men would spend their time, knew that he must have more defense than his fists.

He turned in at the general store and when he came out, he had a new, loaded Colt stuck in his belt under the heavy coat. He felt less helpless now. He walked into the cafe, needing breakfast before he sought Euston and started his grim task.

While eating, he felt someone looking hard and steadily at him. His head idly turned and he saw the girl with the bronze hair standing in the doorway between cafe and hotel. Apparently sight of him had stopped her short, surprise and consternation in her eyes.

They were green, he saw now, a clear, sea-green. Her cheeks planed to high cheekbones that lengthened and pointed the piquant face, framed by the swirl of coppery hair. A touch of high color matched the deep, natural red of the lips. Brant had been right in that brief glance. She was a beauty.

She took a table across the room. Brant watched her graceful walk and proud carriage. Then he tried to give full attention to his problem, sipping his coffee. But his eyes moved slowly and inevitably about the room to the girl.

She ordered, smiling at the waitress, and it gave her a glow of new beauty. Brant finished his coffee and, reluctant to leave, ordered another, thinking that it was still a mite early to find the sheriff. His body ached, the day outside was raw and he wanted to look at the girl. He wondered what she saw in Don Yoder.

The girl finished her light breakfast, paid the waitress and arose. Brant looked down at the table, but from under his brows he saw that the girl swept toward the door. Suddenly she stopped, turned and came directly to him. Brant looked up, surprised.

"You're Greg Avery's brother?" she asked. Her voice was low but not deep.

Brant came hastily to his feet. "I'm his brother, ma'am: Did you know . . ."

"I know why you came to Gunsight, Mr. Avery."

Brant's eyes glinted. "Do you now, Miss . . . Miss . . ."

"There's no place for your kind in Gunsight, Mr. Avery. We've had quite enough shady characters and outlaws." She looked at his bruised face. "I see you've been brawling. That is like your kind. Why don't you leave before you end up as your brother deservedly did?"

Brant stared, momentarily speechless. Yoder had not told her of last night's work, but he had definitely poisoned her against him. He was suddenly so angry that he had to hold his arms very tight to his sides to keep from shaking.

Brant caught his voice. "My kind, ma'am? What kind am I? Who told you?"

"I've heard enough to know," she snapped.

"Now let's see. So far three people have had any talk with me." Brant ticked them off on his fingers. "First there was Tex Euston, and he didn't throw me in jail. There was the lawyer, Larrabee, and he didn't want to bring me into any court. That leaves Don Yoder."

The slight flush in her cheeks told Brant enough. He looked at her in mock surprise and her flush grew deeper. "So it was him. I can't help but wonder why the word of a killer carries so much weight with you, ma'am."

She gasped and her green eyes blazed with a new fire. Her chin set and, before Brant could move, her hand made a sharp crack as it landed on Brant's cheek and mouth in a hard, stinging blow. She whirled about and swept out of the room.

Brant stood there, his cheek stinging. The waitress stood a table away, her reddened face a round mirror of surprise. The few other people had turned about in their chairs to look in curiosity and amazement. Brant's face flamed and he hastily picked up his hat.

"Who was that girl?" he asked as he paid the waitress.

"Helen Dahl. Her father is manager of Spade Ranch."

"Spade! No wonder she . . ."

"Mister, you sure used spurs. She's engaged, they say to Don. Yoder."

Brant's lips formed a silent whistle and he rubbed his cheek again. He left the cafe by the street door, still feeling the sting of the slap. He could understand her attitude now, and her loyalty, though he thought it misplaced.

He found Tex Euston seated behind his desk, working his way through a stack of legal forms that he pushed aside when Brant came in. His white brows knotted down as he had a full look at Brant's face. He spoke dryly. "You look like you had a right heavy evening. Anything I should know?"

Brant shook his head, eased down in a chair with a sigh of relief for his twinging muscles. "I met some folks last night. We played a little rough."

"Anyone I know?"

"Might be, but it's over." Brant looked sharply at Tex. "How about the beef they found at Greg's? Any real proof they were stolen?"

Tex spread his hands. "I never saw that bunch of cattle, so I don't know what brand they wore. But Circle C knew about them. I checked that right away. They swore they bore the Circle C brand and that they had disappeared from a holding ground two days before."

"And they were driven back to Circle C after. Greg was killed?"

"Sure, but that's natural enough, Avery."

Brant nodded. "But it sure as hell is an easy way to make Greg a rustler."

Euston sucked in his leathery cheeks. "You're hell bent on making liars out of Circle C."

"Any reason why I shouldn't if I can prove it?"

"That's the point, Avery. Prove it."

"That's why I'm here. What about that property of Greg's? What's happened to it?"

Euston looked blank. "Why, I reckon the place is all closed up. Hey! I reckon you're the heir!"

"Greg was alone?"

"No legal heirs," Tex said shortly, "except you. We'd better see Larrabee right away. All legal matters in these parts are handled by him. I've been wondering what'd happen to that place."

He took his hat from a wall peg and Brant followed him down the street. He looked for sign of Yoder or his riders but saw none. Nor did he have a glimpse of Helen Dahl. It was just as well. The girl would probably slap him again.

They went up the narrow stairs and Euston rapped once on the inner office door and pushed it open. Larrabee swung around from his desk. He saw Brant and there was a flicker of real surprise in his eyes, quickly veiled. He stood up, smiling, extended his hand.

"Didn't expect to see you this soon, Avery."

Brant gave Larrabee a swift, searching glance but the man's smile was open and he waved his visitors to chairs. He sat down in his own. "What can I do for you?"

Euston spoke up. "About that property of Greg's, Jared. Brant asked about it and I reckon he's the one it'll go to."

Larrabee nodded. "Greg never made a will that I know of, though there may be something out at the place. He might have wanted to leave it to Belle Rainey but she has no legal claim on his estate, or on him."

"What about this Belle Rainey?" Brant asked.

Larrabee stirred uncomfortably. "A friend of Greg's."

Brant looked around at Euston, who studied the bindings on a shelf of law books. "That's all?"

"Well, Belle is a good looking woman," Larrabee said easily. "She and Greg sort of — well, liked one another."

"She stayed out there?" Brant asked shortly.

"She stayed there," Larrabee said. "But that has no bearing on the rights to the property."

Brant asked, "Who is this woman?"

Euston sighed, realizing Brant would not be side-tracked. "Belle's Jeff Rainey's sister. She come from up in the hills. Jeff ramrods the wild bunch up there and everytime a steer turns up missing, they're tagged with the rustling. It could be true, I reckon."

"And she was with Greg?" Brant said. "No wonder the big ranches figured Greg was mixed up with them." His jaw tightened. "But I know my brother better than any man."

Larrabee stirred. "Avery, why don't you take over Greg's place? I can take care of the title ransfer."

44

Brant considered the idea. Euston described the place and Brant realized that it was almost in the very center of the area over which he must ride. It would make an excellent base of operations.

"You say Circle C's not far from it in one direction," he said, "and it's not far from the broken country. How about Hinson?"

"Lee's a neighbor," Euston answered. "Hinson spent a lot of time at Greg's store and saloon. There were a lot of other small ranchers figured Greg's place was a kind of headquarters, a near place to get news of one another."

"Must not have been far from where Belle lived," Brant said thoughtfully.

"Close enough," Larrabee agreed smoothly. "But if she's gone back into the hills, you can forget her. I doubt if you'd live long enough up in that country to even get a glimpse of her."

"That bad!" Brant said softly. Larrabee nodded and Brant gently touched his bruised lips. "And Kit Thomas is at Spade. It's not far, either?"

"He was taken there to have a home," Larrabee said flatly.

Euston grunted. "Or to keep him from answering questions. The time I went up there, they had him clean to hell and gone on the far side of the ranch."

Larrabee looked annoyed. "That's a sorry way to look at it, Tex."

"Spade," Brant cut in. "That's where Helen Dahl lives."

Larrabee and Brant looked at him in surprise. Larrabee first caught his tongue. "You've met Helen?"

Brant grinned. "Just this morning. Got slapped, too. Sort of goes with her red hair and green eyes."

Euston chuckled. "It goes with something else. Her Paw is an Association man, and all she knows is that side of the argument. Besides, Don Yoder's been courting her and some say they'll get married. You won't be welcome on Spade, friend."

Brant nodded and turned to Larrabee. "I'll stay at Greg's, at least look it over. You take care of the law part of it."

"I will." Larrabee seemed relieved that the meeting was over. He was on his feet in an instant. "I'll file the necessary papers. There shouldn't be much delay."

Brant took leave of Euston on the street. The sky was slowly losing its steel-like quality and the wind was not as keen as it had been. There was nothing more to hold him in town and the longer he remained, the more chance of running into Yoder. When next he met Don Yoder, he wanted to see the man arraigned before a judge's bench.

Brant went to the hotel and checked out, then to the livery stable where he saddled his horse. He stopped briefly at the sheriff's office, told Euston his general plan to search for the witnesses, to try to reach Kit Thomas.

Euston made a grimace. "I don't know. If word gets around that an Avery has come back to the old place, maybe they'll try to get rid of you like they did Greg."

46

"They might," Brant agreed. "But they'll have to work harder. You could still make me a deputy."

"I could," Euston agreed, "but I won't — not for a while, anyhow." He changed the subject. "When'll I see you?"

"As soon as I've got witnesses who won't be afraid to talk."

"You could grow a hell of a long beard in that time," Euston grinned and extended his hand. "If I don't hear from you soon, I'll ride out to have a look. Just to make sure."

Brant left Gunsight behind and he felt better, as though he now moved toward a definite objective. He breathed deeply, winced at the catch of muscles in his chest. Don Yoder's work!

His thoughts turned to Helen Dahl. He saw her flashing-green eyes, the angry set of the lovely mouth. He saw them all much too clearly for his own peace of mind. He sighed, regretfully. Helen Dahl and Brant Avery were bound to clash and, he knew, she was bound to be hurt if it was true about her and Don Yoder. He wished the girl would not hate him for the rest of her life. He shook his head, knowing this was a useless thought.

CHAPTER
FIVE

Brant rode slowly, shifting in the saddle now and then to ease an aching muscle. His face felt stiff and there was a slight puffiness about his mouth. These would pass, but he determined that in due time Don Yoder would pay for them.

The sun never fully came out. The road was little more than a brown, muddy trail through the grasslands. Brant's practiced eye judged the gently rolling land that lifted to low hills in the north, the plain itself broken ahead by a second line of smaller hills that were hardly more than mounds.

This was good range. The snow and rains would bring up deep, rich grass as the year advanced. He could understand why men wanted this land, why they fought for it. But it was one thing to fight openly; quite another to use every foul means, to suborn legislatures and judges, to resort to ambush gun, to so scorn the law that hired men of the Association could use a hang rope, and still find protection from justice. The thought spoiled the very look of the land. Brant wondered if all of nature's richness had not in itself turned men into wolves and worse.

He came to the low line of hills and the road wound briefly through them. He knew Greg's place lay not far beyond. At last the road made a few final short turns and the hills fell away to either side. The open, rolling country continued to his left and to the south. But just ahead it was pinched into long grassy fingers by the lift of the higher hills and the low mountains that swept around to the right and made dark fingers against the monochrome sky.

Brant's attention centered on a group of low buildings some distance away. The road headed for them in long, lazy curves, like a somnolent snake. Another road led up from the south. He could make out three or four large buildings and then a vague jumble that must be corrals and pens. He pursed his lips in surprise. He had not quite envisioned so large a place. Greg must have done well. Brant lightly touched spurs to the horse and started down the slope.

The wonder at Greg's swift prosperity still nagged at him. He recalled what Larrabee had said and instantly rejected it. Yet his eyes moved to the broken country to the north, the open range to the south, the way the roads met at this particular place. He admitted reluctantly that Greg had picked the perfect spot for such operations.

He came to the crossroads and drew rein. Greg's, store faced him, a two-storeyed building painted a dull white, long and ample enough to contain general store in one half and saloon in the other. The doors were closed and there was a thick layer of dust on the windows. A long hitchrack stood before the high porch of the building.

To the left and sitting far back so that he could see but a corner of the building; was a long, low log structure, obviously Greg's living quarters. It was stoutly built, to withstand the howling blizzards that winters in these parts generated. Brant could see but a section of the corrals, stout, ample — empty.

Brant rode toward the house. As he came around the corner of the store building, he saw more pens, these for cattle. Old sign confirmed the story that they had once been filled. He saw a barn, also constructed of stout logs, with a high pitched roof that spoke of ample loft beneath the shake shingled roof.

Brant rode on to the house and dismounted. Brant walked to the house. His boots echoed hollowly under the low verandah and he tested the door latch. Typical of cow country, he had only to lift the rawhide string, press gently against the thick planks and the door swung open. He again hesitated, confronting the darker interior. He swept off his hat and then stepped inside.

The room was low-ceilinged, long, and there was a sense of not-long departed warmth. Brant's gray eyes moved slowly and somberly from bearskin rug to Indian blanket on the wall, its colors slightly dimmed by layers of dust. He saw the rifle over the mantle, Greg's favorite gun even before he had come to this country. Brant's eyes misted slightly and he moved brusquely into the room, glad to hear the sound of his steps, the jingle of his spurs.

He felt like an intruder, though he knew the house was empty. He eased open a door and looked in on a bedroom. He found other rooms, even a cubbyhole of an office and, beyond the fireplace, a big kitchen where a dark stove gleamed a welcome.

Brant sighed and his glance cut around the room, suddenly rested on a plate on the table. He bent down to catch the light against the glaze of the pottery. It was undimmed by dust. His glance, sharp now, cut around the room. He saw deep cupboards, and flung open the doors.

His eyes swung to the shelves, spotting another dish that had no dust, salt and pepper containers that had eluded the months and remained bright, a few staples that had been recently used. Brant closed the doors, turned slowly and surveyed the room. He strode purposefully out of the kitchen and into the big main room. Now he looked closely for sign. The rawhide seat of the big chair was also free of dust. He placed his hand on it but there was no warmth. He looked at the fireplace. The ashes were gray but, when he crouched before them and held out his hand, he detected a faint trace of heat.

He crossed the room to the office. It looked untouched, dust everywhere, so he went to one of the other rooms. It was also untouched and had that subtle air that comes to rooms empty too long. He went to the next room.

He looked at the dresser top, the single straight chair and saw that they also lacked the film of dust. Then he noticed wrinkles in the gray blanket that covered the bed, the pillow slightly out of line. Brant had the feeling that this was Greg's room, though there was the aura of a more alien presence. He walked to the chest of drawers, hesitated and then almost jerked open the top one. With a twist of pain, he recognized the tie pin that Greg always wore, the hair brushes, the silver along the edge of one slightly scratched so that the yellow brass showed beneath the plating. He could almost see Greg standing before the mirror, smoothing back his raven hair.

Brant opened the second drawer. Greg's clothing, shirts — nothing more. He opened the third. It was almost empty except for a ribbon, a brooch, a rhinestone setting gone. Belle Rainey's? Brant wondered and he half turned to look at the room again, picturing a woman here. He closed the drawer, thinking this was something personal to Greg.

He walked to the window and looked out. His view was almost directly toward the jagged fine of the hills. This woman had come to Greg from out of those hills and she had returned to them. What knowledge had she taken with her?

Brant restlessly crossed the room and stood outside on the verandah. His eyes moved to the silent store building, the empty corrals and then centered on the barn. He loosened his Colt in the holster and walked tense and alert toward the building.

He paused before the wide, closed doors, then slowly drew his Colt, whipped one of the doors open and jumped back. There was no challenge, no sound. He waited, senses keening into the shadowy interior. The silence was truly empty. Yet he held his gun ready when he stepped inside. Greg had built solidly and well, that was evident wherever Brant turned. But now he was more alert for the little, half hidden sign. He found it on one of the stalls. A horse had been here within the day.

So Greg's place was not deserted. He wondered if his arrival had driven the intruder off. Don Yoder? Brant looked up toward the loft, at the black square of the opening. There was no sense of watching, unseen eyes. Brant rejected Yoder, feeling that the man would have long since sprung the trap.

Brant then strode out into the yard. He threw a quick glance to the boundaries, the line of bushes and small trees on one side, the corrals hemming in a second, the house and the store to the east and southwest. He turned across the yard to the long store building. He circled it to the front, making no attempt to walk silently. His boots echoed hollowly on the long verandah and he tried the front door with a firm rattle of the lock. The dust on the glass was thick and he could only vaguely make out the interior. Brant circled the building again and tried the wide back doors, obviously used to receive shipments from huge freight wagons. They were barred from within.

He walked along the length of the building to the far corner. He saw a small, narrow door here and he tried the knob. It swung inward at his touch, revealing a narrow, short passage ending at another closed door.

Brant hesitated. His fingers touched the handle of the Colt and his eyes narrowed. Then he deliberately thumbed his hat back and pushed the door open with his left hand, keeping his right close to the holster, the thumb hooked in the belt just beside the buckle.

He looked into a long and narrow room, saw the three card tables, the empty chairs, the windows beyond. A partition cut the room and a low, narrow door gave access to the store in the other half of the building. Again Brant sensed honest, emptiness. He stepped into the room. His glance cut to the dust-tinted light that came through the big windows, then to the dark, heavy bar, the mirror behind it, the bottles . . . His eyes came instantly to rest on three objects on the bar.

A whiskey bottle stood there, stoppered, a little over three-fourths full. Beside it sat an empty shot glass and, just beyond, a minute mound of ash, as though someone had smoked as he drank.

Brant bent to catch the light on bottle and glass. No dust. He looked into a tarnished spittoon at the base of the bar and saw the shredded remnants of a cigarette. Brant's fingers lightly drummed on the bar. He grinned, circled the bar and found another shot glass. He filled it from the bottle, lifted it to the dusty windows.

"To you, friend, may you learn to cover a trail somewhere between here and hell."

He drank, slapped his glass beside the other. With new determination, his gray eyes alight and sharp, he retraced his way down the short passage and outside. His horse looked around, then patiently drooped its head again. Brant whistled, the sound carrying loud and clear. He took his time crossing the yard, even climbing the top rail of one of the pens. He made a show of looking around, down the road that led to the valley, a longer time at the dark frown of the hills to the north. He was clearly lined against the sky.

Satisfied, Brant jumped down and, still whistling, picked up the horses's reins, swung into the saddle. He touched spurs to the horse, neck reined about and ambled slowly out of the yard.

At the edge of the road, he pulled in. He twisted about and studied the jumble of buildings and pens. He finally turned south down the road. Tangled brush and small trees at one point touched the trail. He reached the woods, rode on without a glance. Beyond, the road curved to the left placing, the tangle of limbs and brush between him and the distant buildings. Brant set the spurs and headed the horse toward the brushy cover.

He made a huge circle, doubling back. He avoided the thicker tangles but still used every bit of cover that he could. He drew rein, sat very still watching his back trail. Satisfied that no one followed, he continued his wide, circling course.

Half an hour later, now north and west of Greg's place, he came on a swale free of brush and turned into it. The grassy trough led eastward and was well hidden by the bush on either rim. Brant finally drew rein, slid out of the saddle and climbed the eastward slope. He found a thick barricade of growth that would take an axe to penetrate. Satisfied, he returned to his horse, now grazing. Brant set himself patiently to wait.

After about three hours, he climbed in the saddle again, rode back down the swale, then took a northward course. The brush gave way to open, hilly country. Brant turned sharply to the right and drifted southward. His hand was never far from his gun and his eyes constantly swept the open glades.

Soon he drew rein. Greg's place must be just ahead, though a tangle of bushes still hid it. Brant checked his gun, replaced it in the holster. Brant removed his hat and slowly edged forward, peering around the corner to the house. It, too, looked empty but he had no real assurance of it. Brant could see nothing else but to take the gamble since he had to reach the interior of the barn.

He crouched low, knowing the pens would give him protection for the first few feet of his dash. He whipped along the front of the barn, ducked within the door, jerking it shut behind him.

His gun was in his hand and he threw a swift look around the stalls. He heard a stir in one and a white-blazed horse looked at him in mild curiosity. Brant grinned in tight triumph then whipped around to the door again, cracked it a trifle and peered toward the house. If the owner of the horse was there, he made no sign.

Brant at last permitted himself the luxury of a soft sigh of relief. He strode down the straw-filled aisle and halted before the stall that held the horse. A saddle hung from a nearby peg. Someone had come to stay for a time.

56

Brant returned to the door and studied the house, the tangle of pens, the silent store. Brant could not easily risk a bullet if he tried to reach either building, nor could he be sure in which one the mysterious intruder waited.

He turned slowly, looked around. He saw the black square of the open trap to the loft, the ladder nailed against the rear wall. His eyes lighted and, in a moment, he had climbed up. He made himself comfortable at the edge of the trap where he could see the lower floor. He again set himself to patient waiting.

Then he heard a faint sound and he came to his feet, crouched, peering down. The Colt slid into his hand and he waited. One of the big doors opened and a shaft of light played along the passage. Steps sounded and a man came into view, strangely foreshortened from Brant's angle. He wore no hat and Brant saw first a thick covering of wavy, black hair. The man spoke to the horse in a surprisingly gentle voice. He turned and Brant glimpsed a big, round dark face, the ridge of a nose that looked Indian.

Brant also saw his cartridge belt, the handle of a gun in the dark, smooth holster. Brant's position up here was awkward. He could not descend without alarming the man, he could not throw a gun on him and then descend the ladder without giving the stranger a chance for his own gun. Brant eased back on his heels and waited.

The big man took care of his horse, gave the animal a final, gentle stroke on the nose, and strode to the door. The second he heard it shut, Brant whipped down

57

the ladder and cat-footed swiftly along the aisle. He eased open the door, his Colt levelled. The stranger was but scant yards ahead. Brant's voice cut the stillness like the "thunk" of a striking knife.

"Stand hitched and lift 'em!"

The big man jerked to a halt as though he had walked into a wall. His heavy arms shot upward and, on Brant's curt order, he slowly turned. His dark eyes found Brant and his swarthy face visibly paled.

"Greg! But you're . . . !" He caught himself and his eyes widened, lighted, and the full lips suddenly broke in a wide grin. "You're — Brant. Greg was always talking about you."

Brant's gun didn't waver. He eased away from the door, alert. "You knew Greg? Maybe you helped hang him."

"Me!" the man exclaimed. He started to lower his arms but the slight move of Brant's gun checked him. "Me — hang Greg! I'm Jim Wolf."

This was one of the missing witnesses. The man who had fled the country months before. Wolf's voice lifted in a new elation. "I'd hoped you'd come, Mister." His eyes cut to the Colt that threatened him, up to Brant's face again.

"Don't use that gun on me, Brant. Use it on the bastards who strung Greg up!"

58

CHAPTER
SIX

The man's bold, black eyes were eager. He was actually fat, although it took a good second look to reveal it. His nose was hooked, and on each side ancient scars cut diagonally toward the jawbone. But they gave him a dashing and adventurous, rather than sinister, look. A thin black mustache adorned the full upper lip.

He grinned now in pleased welcome. Brant studied the wide shoulders, the deep chest that sloped into a decided paunch. His cartridge belt was old, but the leather had the soft and pliable look that bespoke care. The Colt held a glitter and the plain walnut handle was smooth.

"Jim Wolf," Brant said. "I heard you'd left the country."

"I had." His eyes dropped to the levelled gun. "A thing like that in a man's face makes him nervous."

Brant half lifted the gun and then, in a swift swing, dropped it into the holster. Wolf's grin widened and he heaved a deep sigh of relief. He pulled out a bandanna and swiped it across his cheeks.

"I need a drink, Avery. Maybe you could stand one?"

Without waiting, he started to the house. Brant followed him. Wolf walked lightly for so heavy a man, and Brant sensed he could move with amazing speed if he so desired. Brant's right hand did not swing far from his gun.

But they were soon in the kitchen and Jim reached into a cupboard to bring out a whiskey bottle and glasses that he placed on the table near the window. He lacked up a chair and motioned Brant to do the same. He filled the glasses, lifted his in salute.

"To Greg Avery — wherever he is."

Brant grimly lifted his glass and drank. He looked about the room, back to the big man again. "What are you doing here? They said you'd left."

Jim Wolf shrugged his beefy shoulders. "I was with Greg so long that this is the only place I call home. Sure, I left. Went to Idaho on a ranch job."

"A long way."

"Too long," Jim agreed, "and I sure as hell didn't like it. So, I come back. I ain't told anyone yet. Sort of thought I'd take a quiet pasear first."

"Why?"

Jim licked his lips and spread a big hand, palm up. "It could be unhealthy if I just come in blind. Things have happened."

"I know," Brant said dryly. "That's why I'm here. I intend to get the men who killed Greg."

Jim's fist slammed the table and his black brows lifted. "By God! I knew it! Greg talked a heap about you, Brant. His lad brother . . . I've heard that a hundred times. From what he said, I figured sooner or later those devils would be fighting an Avery again."

60

"They will be. I'll have them in jail or strung up by the law before this is over."

Jim nodded and then doubt came in his eyes. He frowned. "In jail? hung by the law?" He shook his head. "Not that bunch. They swing too much power in these parts."

Brant smiled tightly. "Right now, maybe. But what happens when they're forced to face trial for murder? What happens when witnesses tell what they know? Even a crooked judge can't buck evidence and a straight jury."

Jim rubbed his hand along his jaw. "I don't know, Brant. I don't think it'll work."

"It takes only witnesses . . . The kid I've heard about, this homesteader, Lee Hinson. You saw the hanging."

Jim's head lifted in frightened surprise. His eyes slid away toward the window. "I never saw the hanging, and there ain't anything I could tell in court."

Brant leaned forward, hands gripping the table. "Wolf, you're lying."

The big man's face froze and his hands doubled into fists. He half rose from his chair. "I don't like a word like that, Avery."

Brant looked calmly up at him. "I don't either, Jim. But you were here when it happened. So you must know something. You weren't blind and you weren't deaf." Brant shrugged. "Now you'd better put a name to it."

Wolf towered above the table, brows knotted. Very slowly the pressure left his lips and the whiteness receded from his knuckles as his fingers uncurled.

"Jim, you thought a lot of Greg?"

"He was always one to ride the river with," Wolf replied without hesitation. "No better man."

"Then do something for him," Brant said sharply. "Tell me the truth and then tell it to Tex Euston and Jared Larrabee."

Jim slowly sat down. He poured a drink, studied the golden brown liquid and then suddenly tossed it down. "You're asking me to kill myself, Brant."

Brant said nothing. Jim squirmed and made a grimace. "Look, Brant, I didn't leave because I *wanted* to go to Idaho. I was told to, or find myself planted in the ground beside Greg. They put money in my pocket and told me to git. They said a job was waiting for me — it was. They said to stay in Idaho."

"Who?"

"Ray Carter and Don Yoder."

"Why did you come back?"

"Well, I didn't like it Idaho way. Didn't like the ranch, the towns, the people. I had to come back to these parts." He shrugged again. "I figured maybe things had blown over. Anyhow, something kept pulling me back."

"Conscience," Brant suggested.

"Now that's something I never had," Jim said sardonically. "It's just — well, folks I know are here. I figured I could slip in, keep low until I found out how things were. If they were still touchy, I could scoot out. If they weren't, maybe I could get a line on some deal."

"When did you come here?"

62

"Two days ago. I watched the place a couple of days before that and saw no one. I thought Greg wouldn't care if I bunked here. I didn't know you'd come. I watched for some of Rainey's boys to wander down from the hills. They always have something going."

"Rainey," Brant said slowly. "There was a Belle Rainey. What about her?"

Wolf grinned. "Mister, you never saw a woman like Belle. Made you hungry just to look at her, but it was no use sashaying 'round. She stuck close to Greg and he was crazy about her. He'd get mad to see another man look too long at Belle — and it was hard not to."

"She'd be up in the hills now?"

"With her brother, Jeff," Wolf nodded. "Nothing to hold her in these parts now Greg's gone. Jeff Rainey and Greg had a working agreement. That's how Greg and Belle happened to meet."

Brant asked the question in a low voice. "Rustling? I hear Rainey's not careful about cows and brands. He worked for Greg?"

Jim Wolf looked down at his empty glass. Brant caught his sharp and penetrating glance. Jim rubbed his finger along his mustache and suddenly arose, walked to the window and looked out on the empty road.

Brant stirred restlessly. "I asked a question."

Jim did not look around. "How do you look on a vented brand?"

"Someone else's cow — not mine," Brant answered readily. "But we're talking about Greg."

Jim swung around. "We're talking about him. There's no point in riding a wide circle around it. You'll get it sooner or later. Greg worked with Rainey, and Jeff took any cow he happened to come across. Greg bought 'em and didn't ask questions."

Jim came back to the table and leaned across it, looking down at Brant. "Hell, man! You know what Greg was like! Always ambitious, always wanting to make extra dollars. Talked wide and free and handsome."

Brant's fist smashed on the table. "I didn't know Greg! Not that one! Greg was always honest, a big man! a better one than me every way from the jack! But this . . ."

Jim straightened, sighed. "But you know how he was," he insisted. "Greg wanted to be big and rich. And here in Gunsight, if you ain't an Association man, you get rich just one way. You pick up all the beef you happen to run across and hope no one's looking."

"Rustler!" Brant breathed.

"Hell, Brant! Big ranchers all over this country got started with a rope and a straight iron. Greg was no worse . . ."

"Get out, Jim," Brant said with sudden, quiet fierceness. "Get out and leave me alone. Greg was no worse — but he was no better. How would you feel if you find your brother was a rustler and . . ."

He broke off. Jim looked blank, shrugged. "I reckon when you come down to it, I'm a rustler, too. Never thought much about it."

"Get out!" Brant snapped, his hand dropping to his holster.

64

Jim looked at his drawn and tortured face, the muscle jumping in the lean cheek, the gray eyes cold and slitted. The big man looked puzzled, a little hurt. "You mean get out for good, Brant?"

"I don't know! I want to think." His voice dropped. "Don Yoder hung Greg. But you just killed him yourself."

"Me! All right, Brant," he said at last. "I answered your question." He walked to the door, turned. "But you can always figure this, friend. I didn't argue Greg into what he did. That was his own say-so. If he was all you said, how come he threw in with Rainey?"

Brant raised his head and his eyes were like cold muzzles of twin Colts. Jim whipped about. Brant heard his steps in the short hall. Then the outer door slammed and Brant was alone.

He sat motionless and the silence of the room had weight, a harsh pressure. Brant looked out the window, aware only of the rectangle of dusty, golden light, not seeing it, his brain numb. Then, slowly, the harsh truth about Greg became a reality and Brant closed his eyes, tightly.

Greg Avery was a rustler. Don Yoder had been right, the whispers had foundation. Jared Larrabee had spoken the truth, and it had all been confirmed by a fat ridge runner. Greg Avery bore the outlaw brand. It was true, it was real. It would remain.

Brant shivered. Face it, Brant Avery. Get it deep in your brain. You haven't got a single reason to stay here another minute. Let Greg's shame be buried with him.

Let the hang-noose tell it all, the bitter truth. You can't change it.

Only then he started to shake. It became apparent in the slight quiver of his chin, the pull of his lips, the clenching of his fingers before they went slack again. Big, laughing, lovable Greg had become a part of the lowest form of range life. Brant, forget you ever had a big brother you worshipped. Let the dream and the fact remain buried in a grave.

Then he saw Don Yoder's dark, taunting face, the arrogant pull of the lips. He saw himself again riding in the wet night, felt the slash of the coiled lariat, the mud forced into his mouth and eyes. Such a man had hung Greg.

Brant's cheeks flamed. He had received the same kind of treatment that Greg had. Not a hangnoose, but the same self-sufficient, arrogant flouting of every man's right. Greg might have been a rustler, but he had been hung out of hand because Don Yoder alone had decided such was the case. There had been no mercy, no justice — a hang rope, the gallows brand.

In like manner Brant had received a brand. He was a kill-seeking brother of a rustler. He had come to murder, to kill. So Don Yoder had decided, and once again no one but Yoder would have a chance to judge. Suddenly Brant heard Euston's worried voice. Big ranch against small; powerful man against those who had to claw for their very existence; the power of the mighty used to make justice a farce. Brant saw Don Yoder clearly as the symbol and tool of such forces. He had been shaped by them, he would be used by them.

Brant's thoughts veered, took a new and unexpected turn. If this was true, then there was more, far more, involved than the hanging of a rustler. This was but part of a dark and evil design that held this land. Brant not only had reason to stay to even the score for Greg, but for the even better reason that no man could stand by and let greater wrongs go unchecked.

Yoder flouted the law. He represented powers above the simple rules of justice and fair play. Greg's killing drove that point home. There had been no trial. Maybe such a trial might have proved beyond doubt what had been hinted before and what Jim Wolf had just confirmed. Brant would have no argument if Greg had been forced to pay for crimes deliberately committed.

A new thought struck Brant. Larrabee had spoken of rustling, but the man had made no direct accusations. Jim Wolf, on the other hand, had been quite explicit. It occurred to Brant that he had accepted the word of a man he had known but a few moments. There had been no real proof. Jim was fearful of Yoder. Had he built up a structure of lies to support Yoder's reason for the lynching? Did Wolf think this might persuade Circle C to allow him to remain in the Gunsight country now that he had returned?

Brant's hand struck the table and he arose. He strode out into the yard and his gray eyes quickly cut about the tangle of pens, searching for the big man. Jim was not in sight.

Brant quickly crossed the yard to the stable. The door was open and Brant stepped inside. The horse was gone and Brant stood for a moment, eyes shadowing, thoughtfully licking his lips. So Jim Wolf had slipped out!

Brant strode out into the yard. He'd trail Jim and bring him in to tell his story to Euston and Larrabee, if he had to use the threat of a gun. He looked beyond the pens to the silent lift of the hills. Wolf could only seek refuge there.

Brant turned to the store, walking now with the firm step of a man who knew what he must do. He entered the store, saw the small rack of guns in the shadows near the saddles and coiled ropes. He considered the weapons a moment and then lifted one down.

A thin film of dust dulled its dark finish. He glanced at the others and was satisfied with his first choice. He would need a long-range, powerful weapon if the stories about the hill outlaws were true. He turned to the dusty shelves and soon found a stock of shells. He broke the boxes and filled the rifle chamber, then a pocket. He checked the loops of his gunbelt.

There was a slight sound across the room and Brant's head jerked up. A large man was framed in the door and, just behind him, stood a girl. Brant stared in surprise. He had seen the girl before, near Larrabee's office.

The man smiled. "Avery? Brant Avery?"

He had a powerful jaw that the smile could not entirely soften. His eyes were a chilled blue and Brant wondered if they had ever warmed. He was portly, but his shoulders were wide and powerful. His hat was pushed back and Brant had a glimpse of gray-streaked, black hair as the man, smile widening, stepped into the room.

The girl followed and Brant's attention swung to her. Her eyes had a deeper blue than the man's and there was a sultry shadow of a pout to her full lips. Her hair was raven black.

Then further movement in the door swung Brant's attention away from the girl. Two punchers came in, thumbs hooked conveniently close to their holstered Colts. Brant recognized the foremost as one of the men who had been with Don Yoder. He whipped around to face the older man hand, his hand slashed to his gun.

The man's laughter checked Brant. "Now, Avery, don't go slapping at the wind. Don't lose your head like my foreman did."

"Your foreman?"

The man nodded. "Don Yoder. I'm Carter — own the Circle C."

Brant realized he was trapped. Carter was with two of his riders, who would not hesitate to gun him down. Brant wondered how many more were outside. Maybe Yoder's session would be child's play compared to this.

Yet why was the girl here? Who was she?

CHAPTER
SEVEN

Carter easily turned to make sure his men had control of the situation. Each had moved to one side so that Carter and the girl would be out of line of fire. They watched Brant, quietly, but there was a definite warning in their level gaze. Carter faced Brant again.

"Heard you might be here, Avery. Wanted to talk to you and I figured this would be a quiet place."

"You and your boys sure like quiet places," Brant said evenly. "Like a canyon where you can hang a man and no one interferes."

Carter made a grimace. One of the men shifted angrily but Carter threw him a swift, warning look. The man subsided. Carter looked at the rifle lying across the showcase, the shell boxes still open.

"I hope you don't aim for trouble, Brant." He lifted his hand as Brant started to answer hotly. "Not that I blame you, understand. But I figure you'd give anyone a chance to explain his side of the story."

"How about Greg? He had no chance."

"I know, and I wish I could do something about it," Carter admitted. He looked toward the partition that divided the store from the bar, then back at Brant. "Avery, you can lose nothing but time listening to what

70

I have to say. Why can't we be comfortable and talk this out fair and square?"

Brant nodded curtly. "We'll talk." His eyes cut to the two riders. "How about your gundogs? Are they here to make sure I say what I'm supposed to — and no more?"

"No," Carter said reasonably. "I didn't know what you'd do when we first met. They were to make sure you'd listen to reason and not make a gun play. Blame me?"

"Not at all."

Carter spoke over his shoulder. "Joe — Crane, get outside and stay there until I call you."

One of the men made an impatient sound. "But, Ray, you can't tell about . . ."

"Wait outside," Carter snapped and his tone brooked no argument. The two men turned and walked out. Carter looked questioningly at Brant. "Well?"

"The lady?" Brant asked. "Can't figure why she's here."

The girl flushed slightly but her violet eyes held Brant's. He thought he detected a faint stir of animosity far down in their depths, but her olive face remained impassive.

Carter grinned. "This is my daughter, Lois. She's along for no reason except she happened to be riding with me — and I don't hide anything from her."

Brant sardonically touched the brim of his hat. "A pleasure to meet you, ma'am. Leastways, I've got a look at Circle C."

"Avery," Carter's voice held a sharp tone, "Lois doesn't have to be here. You act like you expect some sort of tricky business on my part. Get it out of your mind. Does she stay — with your permission — or not?"

Brant felt as though his knuckles had been deservedly rapped. He swept off his hat. "My apologies, ma'am. I'd like you to stay."

Carter nodded, pleased, crossed the room, the girl following him, her eyes never leaving Brant. He considered the rifle still lying across the counter. With an impatient gesture, he circled the counter and followed the Carters into the other section.

Carter stood before the bar. His daughter had moved to the window and she looked curiously about as though it was the first time she had ever been inside a saloon. Carter made a gesture toward the dusty bottles behind the bar. "It's your stock, Avery. You pour the drinks. It's on me."

Brant smiled tightly. "Your mistake, Carter. It's on me, like Greg played host to a party once."

He deliberately ignored Carter's sharp look and the slight hiss of the girl's indrawn breath. He selected a good brand, found shot glasses and filled them. He looked inquiringly at Carter.

"The table by the window," Carter said shortly.

Brant took the glasses to the table. He pulled back a chair and looked inquiringly at Lois Carter, who hesitated a second then, chin lifting, sat down with a rustle of skirts. Carter pulled out his own chair and

Brant eased into another where he could watch both father and daughter.

Carter took a sip and then put it down as though the whiskey, for all its quality, did not quite meet his taste. Lois sat with her hands in her lap, her eyes resting steadily on nothing across the room. Carter cleared his throat.

"Look Avery, I know what you're thinking. I don't blame you. But you have no cause to believe I plan you any harm."

Brant started to reply but Carter's swift gesture cut him short. "Listen, and then have your say. I heard you came to town and I wasn't surprised. If Greg had any relatives; they'd show up sooner or later. Circle C hung your brother. I admit it. But I also tell you right now it wasn't on my orders. I want you to believe that."

Brant's brows bracketed and his dark face looked satanic. "It was a mistake? Kind of permanent for Greg, wasn't it?"

"No one knows that better than me. It's given me a hell of a lot of bad nights and black thoughts." He hitched forward. "I wanted Greg brought in and turned over to the law. That's straight!"

"But he wasn't," Brant said.

"I know!" He glanced appealingly at his daughter who continued to gaze at a spot on the far wall. "I questioned my boys mighty close about what happened. They said Greg used the dirtiest language you could hear this side of hell. He swore he wouldn't come along with them to the sheriff and, when the boys kept after him, he started a fight. I don't know what you might've done in a spot like that. My boys had been called every name in the book and then Greg wanted gunsmoke. He made that kind of a play. My boys lost their heads and by the time they got some sense back, the job was over." Carter sighed. "Nothing. could've been done about it then."

Brant listened, his face a mask. He threw a covert glance at the girl and caught her violet eyes on him for an instant before they jerked back to the wall.

Brant stirred. "You make it sound reasonable. Point, is, I don't swallow it."

"Now wait, Avery. I knew the boys were wrong. I made 'em ride into town and give themselves up."

"To Tex Euston or to your own judge?" Brant asked.

"They had the best legal advice," Carter snapped.

"Whose?"

Lois Carter looked at Brant, cold and haughty. "You question my father?"

Brant grinned at her sheer effrontery, gave her a mocking nod. "Maybe not in front of his daughter, ma'am. But it is a point to wonder about."

"Anyhow, they surrendered themselves," Carter snapped. "I didn't want trouble but I couldn't help it. I did what I could to make things square with the law. I want you to understand that."

Brant's voice chilled and his gray eyes grew icey. "Now, let's come to me." He touched his bruised face. "The first night I was in town, I had visitors. Don Yoder and some of your boys made a committee to take me out of the country. They used fists and a coiled lariat to make sure I understood."

74

Carter stared, eyes rounding. Lois lost her aloofness, and Brant was not so sure that either of them knew what had happened. Carter spoke first. "Don! Some of the others!"

"One of 'em's with you now. The man called Joe."

Carter studied Brant and then, without a word, pulled himself from the chair and walked deliberately around the partition. Brant heard his voice, muffled in the narrow hallway, call to someone in the yard. He returned to the barroom, picked up the bottle Brant had left on the bar and brought it to the table. Shortly, the man called Joe appeared. Carter beckoned him to the table, settled down in his chair and gave the man a piercing study.

"Where were you last night, Joe?"

"In town."

"Doing what?"

Joe glanced at Brant, shrugged. "Telling this jasper Gunsight range ain't a good place for Averys."

Carter's fist banged on the table and his shot glass jumped, spilled. "Who in blazing hell told you to do that?"

Joe was surprised. "Why, I figured you wanted it that way. Leastways, Don talked like it."

"Don!" Carter snapped. "Jumping in with all feet and not looking! By God, he'll hear about this one! Get the hell out of my sight!"

Brant watched and listened. Carter looked to be thoroughly angry, and the red flamed into his pendulous cheeks. Brant threw a swift glance at Joe,

75

who did not quite take this spurring as an innocent man should.

Brant looked at Lois Carter, and he could tell by the slight shadows in the corners of her lips that she knew he studied her. She was a shade taller than her father and somewhere in the family there must have been Spanish blood. Her head was held proudly and Brant liked the shape of her mouth, the sharp, clean fine of the nose, the sweeping arch of the brows. She sat in the proper manner and yet there was something sensuous about her; in the set of her lips, the depths of her eyes. Her breasts pushed in full mounds against the silk cloth of her prim shirtwaist.

Carter dismissed Joe and swung about to the table. He sighed. "I don't know, Avery. I blame my men, and yet I don't. Damn it! they try to do what they think is best for me!"

"And hard on others?" Brant demanded.

"Avery, let's be reasonable. Maybe it's hard for you to believe that I didn't want any harm to come to your brother. It's just as reasonable for me to think you've come to Gunsight to notch your guns because Greg died."

"It's reasonable," Brant admitted.

"Avery, I've had enough trouble, even if someone else shoves it on me intending to be of help. There's been just too damned much quarrelling, gunplay, trouble, on this whole range. I'm tired of it clean down to my boots. I'm tired of people thinking I have something to do with everything that happens."

"Your men . . ." Brant started.

"My men hung Greg," Carter cut in. "So blame me." He hitched forward. "You were a fair man, Brant, before this thing came up?"

Brant answered slowly. "I'm trying to be a fair man now . . . but it's hard."

"Then you'll understand what I've got to say. I never in my life knowingly hired a gunslammer or outlaw." He lifted his hand as Brant started to protest. "There's a lot more to be said. Gunsight is trouble range. It was in the old days when Red Cloud and his Sioux were kicking up all the dust. It has been since."

"Meaning you *have* to hire gunmen," Brant said with sharp sarcasm.

"Meaning nothing of the kind! I have to have men who can take care of themselves. There's not a man on my payroll who wouldn't go through the ranges of hell for Circle C."

Brant stirred but Carter continued to speak incisively. "I back them, they back me. If one of 'em goes outlaw or takes to the gun, I tie a can to his tail. But if they make a mistake, believing they're doing something for me or the spread, I back 'em."

"Even to a hanging!" Brant exclaimed.

Carter took a deep breath. "Greg asked for what he got. He could have kept his mouth shut and his hand away from his gun and he'd have had a trial. He didn't. My boys figured he had rustled my beef. Circle C is their spread and it had been robbed. What the hell could I do but see that they get the best lawyers and a fair trial when it comes up?"

"Will it?" Brant asked.

"Have you heard of anyone trying to stop it?"

Brant started to make a hot reply and realized the futility of it. Either Carter was honest and did not know what had been going on, or he was as tricky as a grizzled mountain lion and just as dangerous. Brant eased back in his chair, his face a mask.

"Avery, maybe I'm loco to come to you like this. But I think I'm talking to a reasonable man."

"Within reason," Brant said.

"Then I'll tell you straight off, I like the way you headed in here the minute you learned what had happened to your brother. You're not a man to sidestep when the chips fall down. You want to do something about him — right?"

"That's the size of it."

"Then I say go ahead! But will you keep a tight cinch on your patience? Will you let the law deal with those men? Maybe it'll take a long time, but it will come. Ain't that the right way to help Greg?"

"Well — yes."

"I knew you'd see it that way! I've judged you right. Now — while waiting for the trial, I'll make another offer."

Brant studied him suspiciously. "What?"

"You come to Circle C. You work for me. No strings, mind you — none at all. I want you on my payroll."

Brant blinked. Of all things, he hadn't expected this. He didn't answer.

Carter stirred again. "How about it? A fair offer?"

Brant toyed with his empty shot glass. Carter started to refill it but Brant signalled him off. He let the silence build up, skipping over a dozen reasons for Carter's offer, probing at motives and consequences.

"If I don't?" he asked suddenly.

"Well — nothing, I reckon."

"You're certain?" Brant asked flatly.

Carter's head lifted and steel came into his square jaw and a winter-cold invaded his eyes. He nodded. "Nothing, Avery . . . so long as you don't try to gun down Circle C riders or set a bushwhack. Don't stir up things that had best be let alone."

"Join you — or fight you?"

"Did I say that! I've given you an offer. You can take it or leave it. Think it over and make up your mind — take your time. If you turn it down, all right. Just don't put a burr under a blanket. You can be stopped, friend."

He took a deep breath and his eyes locked with Brant's in a naked, harsh challenge. He spoke softly, almost a whisper. "Circle C has a heap of ways of stopping a man."

There was silence again. Brant felt anger rise but he held it in check. He looked out the window, afraid that his eyes or expression would give Carter some clue as to the way he felt.

Lois stirred. "We'd better go, Dad."

"Sure, Lois."

He started to rise but Brant swung about. "You're warning me to watch out for a bullet if I ride the wrong trail?"

Carter spoke harshly. "Call it what you like."

Brant threw the second question, watching Lois rather than her father. "Have you asked Jared Larrabee the legal angles of shooting a man who won't do what you tell him?"

Carter looked blank, but the girl paled slightly and her breath sucked in. For a moment her eyes blazed in anger at Brant, then she turned toward the door. Her posture of indifference was not quite convincing.

Carter shook his head. "Now what in hell has Larrabee to do with this! He'd like nothing better'n hanging a Circle C scalp on his lawyer's diploma."

Carter followed his daughter to the door. She walked on, and in the silence Brant could hear the slight tap of her heels as she crossed the far room to the narrow passage that led to the outer door. Carter, however, swung around in the partition opening.

"You're making some bad guesses, Avery. Don't make the mistake your brother did. In this country, the Association makes its own laws, or puts its own meanings to those on the books."

"From what I've heard, that figures," Brant answered quietly.

"You're no fool, Avery. There's no need for us to circle around with our hackles up like a couple of feisty dogs. I made an offer. Think it over. Ask around what Ray Carter means on this range, how good his word is. Then make up your mind."

"How long?"

Carter shrugged. "Reasonable time — say a week."

"Long enough," Brant nodded, his voice without expression.

CHAPTER
EIGHT

Brant remained seated until he heard the outer door pulled, firmly shut. Then he crossed, to the window, taking position to one side. He could see the junction of the roads and for some distance to either side of the window. He did not have long to wait.

Carter came riding into the road, Lois just behind him, then the two men and, as Brant had suspected, three others. He watched them ride boldly into the road and then along the front of the building.

He drew back so as not to be seen. Carter did not once cast a glance at the windows, but Lois could not quite control her curiosity. She threw a sidelong look at the building as she rode by. Then Brant could see nothing but their backs, swaying to the rhythm of the horses, but even their backs were an epitome of arrogance.

Brant walked back to the table. The whiskey bottle still sat where Carter had left it Brant considered it, then poured a short drink. He sat down, the glass at his finger tips. He shifted to an easier position, tossed down the whiskey and then began to think.

What had happened to Greg? Brant moodily considered the question and then dismissed it. Now he wanted to think over Carter's offer, the implications of it.

Work for the very outfit that had hung his brother! Take orders, no doubt, from Don Yoder! It didn't quite make sense one way. Yet Carter was not a man to say one thing and mean another. Then, why this offer? Brant had detected a ring of sincerity in Carter's statement that he was tired of trouble. Maybe he thought this would be one way of warding off new trouble that must now loom large with Brant's presence. Why need Circle C fear Brant Avery?

Brant's lips formed a crooked line across his lean face. Afraid of Brant Avery! He'd be a fool to think that. Carter thought only that Brant might stir up things. They wanted Greg's hanging to fade gradually in importance. It would not be brought to trial if none pressed. It would be forgotten — softened memories, legal delays, plus the subtle pressure of Circle C, and Association power would do the trick — except that Brant Avery might, challenge that power, and remind the 'little' rancher that he had legal rights.

There lay Carter's fear, if such it might be called. Brant frowned as he concentrated on this line of reasoning. It was why Jim Wolf was hustled off to Idaho, arrogance had exiled rather than destroyed. No wonder Jim Wolf feared Carter, the Association. No wonder witnesses' memories slipped so badly when they might bring Association lead, reprisals such as Brant himself had experienced on that muddy road outside Gunsight.

Brant's jaw tightened and his eyes narrowed. Who in hell did Carter and his bunch think they were! He warned himself to let his anger go by the board. Undoubtedly Gunsight's boothill contained men who had let anger rule them. Someone had to throw a loop over the Association's power. Someone had to force justice down the Association's throat. Maybe Brant Avery was that man. There and then he accepted the job.

He must find those who had actually witnessed the hanging. He must overcome their fear of the wrath of the Association. He must bring them to Larrabee or Euston and have them tell their story. They must be protected until there were enough of them that the case could be brought to trial.

Then he remembered Carter's words. A week — just a week, and he must decide. He actually wouldn't have that long if he made some move against Carter or Yoder. Yet, if he could, manage it, he would have a week of grace — not much, but something.

Jim Wolf — Brant's thoughts swung to the big man. Jim was up in the hills. He knew plenty, if Brant guessed right. If Brant could find him, then the week of grace would be well spent and Circle C would have no idea of his activities. If word spread Wolf had gained courage to stand up against the Association, others might come forward.

Brant crossed the room with long and purposeful strides. He entered, the store side of the building and picked up the rifle. Swept the cartridges into his pockets and then strode down the hall. He came out into the yard, glanced up toward the dull and scudding clouds. Late, but maybe Jim had not gone far, thinking himself safe once he was in the first folds of the hills.

Brant paid a brief visit to the house, getting a few more staples. Then he cast about the yard for a sign. In a matter of minutes he found it and the trail led off toward the north and west. Jim Wolf had certainly gone into the hills.

Brant cut around the barn, found his horse peacefully grazing. He swung into the saddle and headed out of the yard, striking toward the hills. Jim was careless at first because of his haste, but once the bushes and trees screened him from immediate pursuit, he had covered his trail. It faded out completely. He might have headed in any direction. Brant put himself in Jim's place. He would not ride toward the domain of the Circle C, Spade, or any other Association ranch. Almost directly ahead, the dark hills rose and Brant saw them as a refuge for a man who felt himself caught in a trap, who sought escape.

Brant lifted the reins and urged the horse ahead. The land gradually lifted to the higher peaks, dark-humped shapes against the dull sky. They formed a maze of twisting canyons, little meadows, confusing passages, as if Nature had forseen this would be cattle country and had deliberately shaped a refuge for rustlers, outlaws, and brand blotters. Greg could not have chosen a better place for his store, saloon and corrals if they were to be a cover for stolen beef. Brant pushed down the sharp hurt the thought evoked, and set his mind to the task of finding Jim Wolf.

84

Within a short time he again drew rein at the mouth of a canyon. Grass hid any sign but, just within, the greenery gave way to bare rock and clay. Brant rode slowly forward, eyes casting sharply about. He studied the ridges, the out-croppings of rock, not sure but that the unknown Rainey may have placed men up there to check such stray riders as Brant.

But he saw no slight stir that might have been a warning, no false shape to rock, or crest or bush that might have disclosed a look-out. Satisfied at least on this point, his eyes cast ahead, sweeping from wall to wall. Almost immediately, he saw the imprint of a horseshoe, then nothing more for several yards where rock again spread across the canyon floor. But beyond he found more prints, fresh. Brant had no need to watch trail now, so long as the precipitous walls forced his quarry on ahead of him. Brant increased the horse's pace, but his eyes never ceased to scan the canyon walls, the rims, the turns ahead that might lead him into any kind of a trap.

Nothing broke the silence. With each turn he came only onto another stretch of the canyon, and he began to wonder if this narrow passage threaded the whole range without a single side canyon. The deeper he penetrated, the deeper the silence. Brant could hear only the soft slur of his own horse's hoofs.

All sign disappeared and was not repeated. He watched the ground, but he also never stopped casting quick glances around the rims. There was no alarm, no warning shot, no movement. He realized he must still be some distance from the heart of the hills and he wondered at the probable extent of this broken country. No wonder Euston didn't want to ride up here. Brant had an inkling of the enormity of his own task.

Night found him still without sign of Jim Wolf. He ate a scanty supper, quickly put out the fire and checked his horse. He rolled up in a blanket and tried to sleep. Instead, he felt a deep sense of discouragement. He was too much aware, by now, of the immense territory the hills covered. Jim Wolf might be hidden but a stone's throw or many miles away. This could well prove to be a long and fruitless search.

Brant finally drifted off to sleep. The first break of dawn awakened him, and he shivered as he stretched the kinks out of his muscles. The light slowly increased and gradually he saw the close-pressing, secretive hills. Brant studied the slopes and canyons, and the discouragement of the night before returned. He made a small fire and soon had breakfast and coffee. He felt slightly better afterwards, but the hard fact remained that, through ignorance of the country, he had set an impossible task for himself.

He refilled his tin cup and calmly considered the situation. He would be a fool to pit precious time against the tangled secrets of these canyons and mountain trails. He could direct his efforts to other angles, such as the evidence of the homesteader, Lee Hinson, or the boy, Kit Thomas. Sooner or later, Jim or the woman, Belle Rainey, or her brother would come out of these hills. Or he might find some guide who would be willing to mark out the way for him. Brant nodded to himself, looked about at the hills.

"This time you win," he said quietly. "But we won't call it final. I'll be back."

He arose with a new determination and hope. He rolled his pack, brought in the horse and saddled it, fixed the blanket roll behind the cantle. He gave the silent hills another, searching glance. He acknowledged a temporary defeat, then touched the horse with his spurs.

He came out of the hills hours later and saw the open country before him. He drew rein and orientated himself. Greg's place lay in that direction. Spade ranch must lie over there, extending far to his left. Beyond it lay Gunsight. Hinson and the other homesteaders must have their places along those distant lower slopes, their ranges sweeping down to touch the richer grass of the plain.

Brant considered the country ahead and below. He wanted to see Hinson, and then Euston, to learn what the sheriff could tell him about this mountain area. Both were in the same general direction across Spade. He lifted the reins, gave the land another searching glance to set its general features in his mind and then rode down the slope. He made no attempt to find a road, but set himself in the general direction of the lower foothills above Gunsight. The miles passed steadily.

Then he saw cattle grazing along the first gentle slopes of the hills. Hinson's could not be far now and Gunsight must be several miles straight ahead. Brant changed his course, now seeking a road that would lead him to the small homesteads just beyond the fringes of this rich range. He came close to some of the beef and his sharp eyes saw the Spade brand.

So he rode in enemy territory. He thought of Kit and wondered if he. should ride to the ranch and ask to see the boy. He rejected it. If Spade actually held Kit a semi-prisoner, Brant would have no chance to see him unless he brought the law along.

Then he thought of Helen Dahl. This was her home. He saw her as vividly as though she stood before him, the touch of bronze in her hair, the sea-green eyes, even the texture and shape of the lips. She might not be too far away and he was surprised at the excitement the thought raised in him.

He rounded a hillock, saw a narrow road not far ahead. Some distance to his right, three men worked at an open fire. Brant hastily drew back to the shelter of the hill, then eased cautiously forward. Two of the distant figures were men, the third was a girl — or a boy. Brant leaned forward, in the saddle. The trio worked over a small branding fire. They might be rustlers, some of Rainey's wild bunch on a quick raid down from the hills. He rejected that. The trio worked too openly. He was now certain the third person was a boy. It might be Kit Thomas.

He studied them. He'd have no chance riding unseen to the fire. He straightened in sudden hope as the boy walked to the three horses and mounted one. A man swept his arm toward the hill that concealed Brant. The boy immediately circled the fire and came this way.

Brant's gray eyes lighted. This was luck! He'd get a chance to talk to Kit, have his story once and for all. He lifted the reins, then froze as a clear voice spoke sharply behind him.

"Lift your hands! High!"

Brant checked an impulse to swing about. He lifted his hands and, with a slight pressure of his knees, made his horse slowly turn so that he could see who had slipped up so quietly.

Helen Dahl faced him, a Colt held steadily on him. Her eyes were cold and sharp, her lips set in an angry line. She lifted the gun, fired a bullet into the air, and then the muzzle swung back to cover him. Brant recovered from his surprise. He had been thinking of this girl and here she was, but not quite in the way he had envisioned her. He could not fully suppress a wry smile.

Helen frowned and spoke sharply. "You might not find Spade so funny, Mr. Avery."

Brant heard a faint shout from beyond the hill and he knew that the gunshot had alarmed the men. They'd be riding hard even now. Helen tightened the reins in her hand, the other held the big Colt as level and steadily as a man's.

Brant's dark brow lifted. "Is this the way Spade treats chance riders and visitors, ma'am?"

"No" she answered coldly. "But you're hardly either. You came out of rustler country. I've watched you for some time, Mr. Avery. When a chance rider keeps himself hidden the way you've done, I think we have a right to be suspicious."

Brant started to answer but a thunder of hoofs interrupted. Two men raced around the hill, saw Helen and Brant, the girl's gun. Their own guns lifted from the holsters.

Brant was welcomed to Spade.

CHAPTER
NINE

The riders came in like swooping hawks and pulled to a sliding halt, mud and grass spewing as the horses planted their hoofs. Brant sat still, keeping his hands folded on the saddle horn in plain sight.

He could now see the boy was undoubtedly Kit Thomas. The boy stared at Brant as though he looked upon some supernatural visitor His blue eyes were big and round and his face had paled so that the freckles stood out like live splotches.

Helen spoke quietly. "Monte, take his gun."

One of the men circled around Brant and leaned far out of the saddle to lift Brant's Colt from the holster. He hastily reined back and Brant saw the relief in Helen's face. Monte circled wide again and then reined in, levelled Brant's gun, grinning crookedly. "How does it feel, looking in your own shooting iron?"

Brant shrugged. "It's still a Colt held by an Association rider. Nothing new in these parts."

"That's not true!" Helen blazed.

Kit caught his voice. "You even sound like Greg! You look like him. You must be his brother!"

Monte nodded. "Just another Avery hankering for a hang noose. Helen, let us take care of this. Won't take long if you'd just ride toward to house."

"No!" she snapped. "We'll take him to Dad."

Monte spoke impatiently. "Just waste of time. End up same way." He saw her stormy eyes and added hastily, ". . . but it's what you say."

He made a motion down the trail with Brant's gun, an imperious order. Helen spoke to her horse, moving ahead and leading the procession. The riders reined aside and Monte looked sardonically at Brant. "We'll sort of follow you, Avery. We don't want you to swallow our dust."

Brant looked at Kit. The boy still stared in wonder, but he swallowed and Brant saw the shadow of uncertainty and fear touch his freckled face. He dropped back to accompany the two men and Brant spoke softly to his animal and headed it after Helen Dahl.

One of the men spoke gruffly. "Bring up the drag, kid. We don't want any stray dogie in the way if trouble breaks."

They struck at right angles to the direction Brant had been traveling. Helen rode but a few feet ahead, the two men and the boy brought up the rear, and Brant rode alone, the menace of the Spade guns at his back. He rode easily as though this was nothing of importance. He studied Helen, the easy sway of her slender body, the way she held her shoulders against the world with an air of courage. She had the dignity of a queen and,

Brant thought wryly, she was certainly queen of all this range.

He lightly touched spurs to the horse, thinking to move up beside her. Instantly Monte's harsh voice checked him.

"Just ride easy, Avery. You'll ride longer."

Helen threw a glance over her shoulder. "Better follow good advice, Mr. Avery."

They topped a low ridge and Spade headquarters lay ahead and below. Brant saw a network of white stock pens and corrals, barns, workshops, bunkhouse and a big cookshack. Beyond them stood the ranch house itself, a long low building with two wings angling back from the main section. Brant's lips formed a silent whistle.

Helen watched him. "Spade Ranch, Mr. Avery. We like it."

He nodded. "I don't blame you. Took a lot of building."

"A lot of planning and a lot of fighting, Mr. Avery. Yet some people say we don't deserve it."

"They're wrong,", Brant said evenly.

Her brows shot up in surprise. "Now that is a strange thing, from you."

"Fair, that's all." His arm made a sweeping gesture. "Grant your right to every bit of this, it's still no excuse for other things."

"Spade is judge of Spade's actions," she said shortly.

"Now there's the rub," Brant said.

Her chin lifted and she urged the horse on. They rode down the slope. Before long, they followed a beaten track that led to the nearest pens, then threaded the maze of them toward the big ranch yard. Two punchers, breaking a horse in a nearby corral, climbed up on the rail.

"Who's your friend, Monte?"

"Gallow's bait," Monte called.

Helen turned angrily. "No more of that!"

Monte subsided with an under-breath growl. As they came into the yard, Brant saw two men and a woman come out on the porch, indistinct for the moment under the dark verandah. As they came closer, Brant recognized Carter and his daughter. He had the wry thought that these two seemed to get around a good deal — yesterday at Greg's place, today here on Spade. Of course, they were neighbors and probably close friends of the Dahls. The procession rode up to the foot of the steps and halted. Carter stared at Brant, his face hardened in anger. He spoke in a swift, low tone over his shoulder to the other man.

Monte's low growl cut in. "Kit, head to the bunkhouse. This is no place for a button."

Kit wheeled about and rode toward the corral. Brant caught his swift, over-shoulder glance, a strange mixture of wonder, curiosity and pleading, as though the boy tried to make his eyes speak for his tongue. Then a harsh voice from the porch and Brant's attention swung about.

"Where'd you get this one, Helen?"

"Watching Monte's branding fire, Dad." She swung out of the saddle and gave Brant a curt signal to dismount. He took his time about it as Helen walked

94

up the steps and told, her father how she had found Brant. Brant stood beside his horse until Dahl spoke sharply to him.

"Come up here, Avery. Let's have a closer look."

He mounted the steps. Now he could see the strong resemblance between father and daughter. Dahl was taller than Helen, his face thinner, but he had the same cool, sea-green eyes. His hair was thin now and plastered close to his skull, yet Brant could tell that once he had Helen's bronze-tinted, thick locks.

Monte spoke harshly from below the porch. "Need us to watch the skunk?"

Helen turned. "That's all, Monte. We can take care of Mr. Avery."

Carter growled, harsh eyes on Brant. "I reckon I wasted my breath on you yesterday. It sure didn't take you long to forget our pow-wow. Lucky men Lois dropped in for a visit."

"I didn't forget our talk," Brant answered readily.

"Then how come . . . ?"

Brant grinned. "I didn't have much chance to explain. I'm an Avery, and that means I'm wrong as hell before I open my mouth."

"That's not true!" Helen blazed.

"Just what were you doing?" Dahl demanded.

"I took a *paesear* to see what the country's like on my way back to Gunsight. Didn't know this was Spade. I'm sorry I spoiled the range by setting my foot on it."

Helen studied him closely and Carter's eyes showed murky suspicion. Brant waited, knowing none of them believed him and yet willing to meet their challenge and their questions.

Helen first broke the silence. "You were keeping yourself out of sight when I rode up."

"That's right," Brant admitted. "I saw the kid working with your riders and, just before, I saw the Spade brand on a steer. I've heard about Kit Thomas."

"So you want a chance to pump him?" Carter demanded.

Brant looked at him as though the answer was obvious. "That's one way of saying it. Greg was my brother — you keep forgetting it — and the lad was the one who actully saw him hung. Anything wrong in seeing him?"

"From you, maybe."

"Carter, put yourself in my place. If you happened onto someone who could tell you what actually happened to your brother, wouldn't you want to talk to him?"

Carter's glance told Brant he had scored. He pressed on. "All of you think it strange I kept myself out of sight. Talk goes around that it's worth a man's hide to try to reach Kit Thomas. Any wonder I played the cards close!"

Helen's shocked voice broke the silence. "That's not true! Anyone can talk to Kit — at any time! You act as though Spade has something terrible to hide!" She whipped around to her father. "That's a lie, isn't it, Dad?"

Dahl was caught off balance and Carter looked at him with a sudden alarm that Brant did not miss.

Helen, however, took the hesitent silence as confirmation. She wheeled around to Monte and his partner, who still waited just below.

"Bring Kit right away. Let him talk to Mr. Avery."

Monte shot a swift, questioning glance at Dahl. He started to shake his head, caught himself. Carter met the situation quickly.

"Have him brought in, Dahl. I can't see any harm in proving to Avery how wrong he is."

Dahl made a signal to Monte, who turned to the corral. The tension in the group eased and Brant felt slightly safer. Carter rubbed his hand along his chest and then his jaw, considering Brant.

"I reckon I slapped a wrong brand on you too fast, Avery. I'm glad to know you're considering my deal." He glanced at Dahl. "Maybe it'd be better inside?"

Dahl caught the hint and in a short while they sat before a wide, dark fireplace in the main room. Brant waited, keeping his eyes on the ash within the maw of the fireplace but aware that both Carter and Dahl had casually placed themselves to block any sudden move to escape. Soon, muffled steps sounded on the porch and Dahl jerked open the door to admit Kit Thomas.

"Come in, boy," he said as Kit's frightened glance moved from one to the other.

"Yes sir," he said, bobbed his head and took a few shuffling steps within the room. Brant looked up to catch his pleading and frightened look. A hell of a thing, he thought, to put the kid on a spot like this.

Kit seemed afraid to get too far from the door and the comparative safety of the ranch yard. Helen smiled at him and the sudden softening of her face, the warm fight in her eyes, transformed her. Brant caught himself staring and hastily looked away.

Her voice was as warm as her smile. "Kit, we'd like you to tell us about Greg Avery."

"Ma'am!" He was surprised. His glance shot to Dahl, lingered on Carter. He tried to evade it. "But I've told you what I know!"

"Tell it again, Kit. We want Mr. Avery to hear."

Kit licked his lips and his eyes shifted again to Carter and Dahl. He waited for their permission. Carter nodded. "Tell him, Kit. Like you told us."

"Yes, sir." He bobbed his head again. His eyes grew distant as though he dredged something up from memory before he spoke, to make sure he would be letter perfect. Brant managed to keep the suspicion out of his eyes, checking his frown.

"I was working out in the corral," Kit said with a sudden rush of words, then took a breath and continued more evenly as though he had found his memory had not slipped. "Greg was inside."

"Jim Wolf?" Carter asked easily.

"Yes, sir. Jim Wolf was in the barn. Don Yoder and some Circle C men rode up and told me they wanted to look at some calves we'd just got the night before."

"The night before?" Dahl insisted.

"That's right," Kit nodded. "Greg come out of the house just then," Kit continued, and he was mighty mad to see Don and the others. He told them to get out and Don tried to explain they wanted to look at those calves. Greg got madder and told them they couldn't."

98

"Why?" Brant asked sharply.

Kit threw a beseeching look at Carter. He held his head down and the sing-song of his voice grew pronounced. "Don said if Greg had nothing to hide, there was no harm in looking at the calves. Made them all mad, but Don didn't do anything. He just walked to the corral."

Kit caught his breath then hurried on. "Greg drew a gun like he was going to shoot Don in the back. But the others jumped him and Greg fought 'em, cussing something fierce. By then Don saw the brand on the calves — Circle C. He told Greg they'd have to go to the sheriff in Gunsight. Greg tried to grab a Colt, but they wouldn't let him."

"This is gospel true, Kit?" Brant shot at him.

The boy looked miserable and seemed on the point of blurting something, but Dahl snapped at Brant, "Why shouldn't the boy tell the truth!"

Brant felt it was important to prove or break the boy's story here and now. "Where was Jim Wolf when all this happened, Kit?"

"Jim? Why, Jim was . . ." He looked confused aware of Brant's narrowed eyes. His own hardened in childish challenge. "Jim was in the barn."

"He didn't come out?" Brant insisted.

Dahl stirred angrily. "Let the kid tell his story."

"Please do, Mr. Avery," Helen said coldly. Brant subsided, feeling he had too many against him and, considering his own position, he dared not push things too far.

99

Kit recovered his poise. "Jim stayed in the barn. He didn't come out to help Greg. I saw him sneak away." Kit took another deep breath. "Don told the other riders to make sure . . ."

"Belle," Brant cut in. "Where was Belle?"

Kit floundered. "She was in the house all the time. She come out when they started to take Greg away. Don told her she'd better get back inside. Don and the men took Greg away and that was the last I saw him."

Brant covertly watched Carter and Dahl. Both men watched Kit with an intensity all out of proportion to the story They acted like uncles listening to a child recite, worried that he might miss a line or forget the whole.

Lois watched Kit, losing some of her cold aloofness. Brant felt that she heard the story for the first time and that she believed. Helen also listened as intently, nodding now and then as though she heard repetitions that were in themselves proof of the story. Brant admitted wryly that it made sense, it hung together but — it just wasn't true.

"Did you want to come to Spade, Kit?" he asked softly.

Helen stirred. "Of course he wanted to! He'd never had a home. Greg Avery and Belle Rainey were not fit people to look after him. Don persuaded Kit to come over here."

So Yoder had brought the boy! Brant thought. In a way that tied in with the uglier picture that he had from Euston. He looked at Kit. "That's right, Kit? Don brought you here?"

"I . . . well, yes, sir." He did not elaborate but the boy's eyes tried to say much more.

Carter stirred. "Well, there's the story, Avery."

"That'll be all, Kit," Dahl said. "You can get back to the bunkhouse."

"Yes, sir!" Kit practically fled to the door.

Carter leaned back with a soft sigh. His voice was affable and patient. "Now you've heard the story, Avery, as the boy saw it. Satisfied that he told the truth?"

Brant wondered what would happen if he bluntly stated his thoughts. He pictured the extent of Spade, the men whom Dahl or Carter could summon. He glanced at Helen, back to Carter. "I reckon that's it, Carter. At least I've heard what he has to say."

Carter smiled and steepled his fingers. "The kid's story should help you decide about Circle C. Ready to give me an answer?"

Brant glanced at Helen who frowned, puzzled. Lois again disregarded Brant but Dahl watched him with an impersonal interest, as though it did not matter if Brant left Spade on his own or was carted off.

"It's something a man don't hurry," Brant said. "Sure, you've made a fair deal as you see it, and Kit has told a story that listens good."

"What else is there?" Carter demanded.

"The chance to be sure I'm not getting my feet tangled in a loop. I still have a week by your own word. Want to go back on it?"

Carter's lips pouted angrily. "I never went back on my word in my life, Avery! You have a week."

Helen interrupted. "Ray, you'd better tell us what this is all about. This is Greg Avery's brother and . . ."

"A damn' good man," Carter cut in. "I don't blame him for coming up here breathing fire against those who . . ." Carter caught himself. "He figured it was something sneaking and low-down. Can't blame him — neither can you, Helen. But now he's finding out what really happened."

Helen sat erect, intent, frowning at Carter, looking at Brant and then back to Carter. The rancher waved his hand. "We had a talk yesterday morning — out at his brother's place. I told him what I knew about it, and what Don Yoder had told me. Now he's heard Kit. I'm sorry, Avery, but I reckon you'd learn about it sooner or later."

Brant nodded bleakly. "Bound to."

"So he has a week to sign on with Circle C. He's the kind of man I like to have around." He caught Helen's worry and smiled. "Sure, Avery's had hard feelings toward Don, and Don ain't exactly in love with this jasper. But now the truth's out, that'll all be changed. They'll make a good team."

Helen looked at Brant, who met her probing gaze his own eyes steady. "I have to apologize, Mr. Avery. But you can understand why. Spade, Circle C and the others have to be constantly on guard lately. We swear that every homesteader and mavericker in the country is nibbling at our land and herds. My father, Ray Carter and the others built all this up themselves. They want to hold it, rightfully, but the others are envious — those little men, those baling wire spreads!"

102

"Including Greg?" Brant asked.

Helen flushed and bit her lip. "You're Greg's brother and some might say the same breed of cat. But I think and hope you're different. If you are, you can't blame me for including Greg Avery. Your brother certainly did all he could to hurt. us."

"I've heard the talk in town," Brant said slowly, "both sides. I've heard Carter. I've just heard Kit. I've never heard Don Yoder's."

"I have — the full story."

"It's like Kit's?"

"Completely — almost word for word."

Brant nodded, a gesture that might mean anything. He looked at Carter, Helen, then at Dahl and spoke directly to the Spade manager. "Any reason I can't be on the trail to Gunsight?"

Dahl shook his head. "None at all. Unless you'd like to visit a spell."

Brant smiled slightly. "I'd say I'd already done that. Could I have my Colt?"

"Certainly." Dahl arose. "I'll have Monte bring it and your horse."

Helen spoke behind Brant, a touch of tartness in her voice. "We're not robbers, Mr. Avery."

CHAPTER
TEN

Dahl walked out on the porch and called to the bunkhouse. Brant heard the faint reply, and Dahl gave orders to bring horse and Colt to the house. Brant turned to Helen to find her watching him with a faint hint of expectancy.

She smiled. "I'm sorry your first visit was like this, Mr. Avery. I hope to see you here again . . . more at ease."

"Oh, he'll be around!" Carter said heartily.

Brant said noncommital good-byes and walked out to the porch, the rest following. Dahl strode to the corral and talked briefly to Monte, returned to the porch.

"They'll bring your horse in a minute," he said to Brant.

Monte and his partner rode up, leading Brant's horse. Brant descended the steps and Monte handed him the Colt. Brant spun the cylinder, checking the load and looked up to catch Monte's sardonic grin.

"It still shoots, friend," Monte said.

Brant holstered the weapon, swung into the saddle. Carter and Dahl watched him impassively. Such men, Brant thought, would be sheer dynamite as enemies, and he thought what little chance Greg had bucking them. He concealed his thoughts, touched the brim of his hat, and neck reined the horse around. Monte and the other man swung with him. Brant pulled in.

Monte grinned. "Something wrong?"

Dahl spoke from the porch. "They'll show you the way, Avery. Spade is big."

"Damn big," Brant grunted.

"Hell, even bigger'n that!" Monte chuckled. "Let's head out."

Brant smiled at Monte in wry understanding, who grinned in reply. Brant touched blunt spurs to the horse and, riding between the two Spade men, headed toward the main county road. The buildings grew smaller behind them as they traversed a long slope to a low ridge. Just as they reached the crest, Brant pulled in, turned half around so that he could look back on the gigantic spread. Monte waited beside him, his muggy eyes also sweeping over the rich graze and then centering on the great main headquarters of the ranch.

He leaned forward, hands resting on the saddle horn and a touch of awe came into his voice. "You ever seen anything like that, Avery? Anywhere? Ever seen anything bigger — or greater?"

"No," Brant answered.

Monte shook his head in wonder. "I never dreamed a spread could be that big. And it has neighbors as big — like Circle C. It fair takes your breath."

Brant's silence was an acceptance of Monte's statement. yet his face grew grim and his eyes bleak. It was big and it did take his breath — but this very thing had killed Greg. He abruptly reined the horse around.

"Let's get along."

Monte grinned. "Sure — but you'll never forget the look of Spade, friend. And never forget Spade and its neighbors rule the roost."

Soon they came to the main road to Gunsight. Brant thought he would lose his companions here, but Monte and his partner kept along with him as though they intended to take him to Gunsight and might even tuck him into bed. They rode for about three miles and then Monte edged his horse in, forcing Brant to draw rein. Monte pulled makings from his pocket and rolled a cigarette.

"Spade line," he said. "This is as far as we go."

"Seeing me off?" Brant asked.

"Something like that." Monte lit the cigarette and folded his hands. "I wonder where I'll see you next. Could be in the Circle C bunkhouse — could be over a gun sight."

"Depends on how the trail runs."

Monte said sharply," It runs toward Gunsight right now. Better start riding."

"And not come back?"

"Not without an invite." Monte wheeled the horse about and lifted his hand in a mocking farewell. "So long, pilgrim, and keep riding."

Monte's right hand was close to his gun and the threat was clear. Brant touched the spurs gently and ambled down the road to Gunsight. He did not look

106

back and yet he knew that two men had not moved. They still waited and watched.

Brant topped a small rise and dropped down the far slope.

Kit Thomas had lied, he knew it. Kit had been drilled on his story. Helen did not know this, that seemed obvious. What would Kit's story really be? He feared Dahl, he feared Carter, probably every man on Spade. If that fear was removed, would he talk? Brant's jaw tightened. It was time he found some way to slip Kit out of Spade.

It was dusk when he at last rode down Gunsight's street and turned into the livery stable. Afterwards, he strolled slowly to the sheriff's office. Euston looked up and gave a pleased start when he saw his visitor. "Well! You act like you learned something."

Brant dropped into a chair. "Enough for one trip, anyhow." He briefly recited what had happened and Euston listened, arching his brows when he heard Wolf mentioned.

"He's back!"

"Was," Brant nodded. "Might be anywhere by now. I think I'll move out to Greg's place as soon as Larrabee can clear the title."

"Why?" Euston asked sharply.

"I've been thinking about the whole thing, Tex. Maybe Wolf didn't tell the whole truth about Greg. Perhaps Greg did have something to do with the stealing. I don't like the Rainey angle, that's too close to owlhoot, and I don't think Jim Wolf is the kind of man to pass up an easy dollar."

"I'd like to talk to Wolf myself," Euston said.

"You can — just ride up in the hills. That's a mean tangle of country."

"Perfect for rustling," Euston nodded. "No place for a lawman. A bushwhack'd be too easy."

"That's what I figure," Brant said. "If I take over Greg's place, Jim and this Rainey might think I'll play their game. They'll make sure one way or the other."

"When?" Euston asked dryly.

"Jim's a witness. Rainey's sister must have seen the whole deal between Greg and Don Yoder. But she will be hard to reach. Wolf will come around first. Right now he's scared to talk or show himself. Circle C bought him off and sent him away."

"They won't like his coming back," Euston nodded.

"They won't," Brant agreed. "I think I can get Wolf to trust me, persuade him his only real safety is in testifying and putting Yoder and the others away in jail."

"Figures," Euston sighed.

Brant looked meaningly at the sheriff. "Point is, you leave him alone. How about it?"

Euston frowned. "All right, Brant. You play Wolf how you want."

They heard a step on the porch. The door opened and Larrabee stepped in. He halted in mid-stride at the sight of Brant. Then he caught himself and smiled. "Didn't expect you back so soon."

"I've seen enough for one trip. But I've decided to take over Greg's store."

"Brant has an offer to work for Circle C," Euston said.

108

"Carter!" Larrabee acted honestly surprised.

Brant scowled at Euston. "I wonder how he knew where to find me."

"Trailed you?"

"With his daughter? Not likely." Brant recalled the first time he had glimpsed Lois Carter and he grinned at Larrabee. "You're not sparking her and happened to let the story out?"

He meant it in jest but Larrabee's eyes became suddenly frightened and wary. Then he threw back his head and laughed. "Now that's a crazy idea! Think Carter's daughter would look at a poor attorney!"

Brant said nothing but he thought the man's laughter was too loud and too shallow. The lawman wore a strange expression as though he had encountered something startling.

Larrabee spoke easily. "Joking aside, Carter did offer you a job?" On Brant's nod, he shook his head. "Surprising. Did you get around to Spade?"

Brant told of his capture by Helen and what Kit Thomas had said when called to tell his story. Larrabee listened, nodding now and then. "Well, I guess that satisfies you about Kit. Maybe it's not the story you wanted to hear . . ."

"It wasn't the right one," Brant said flatly.

Larrabee stared. "But he . . ."

"He was scared to death," Brant said. He looked at Euston, back at Larrabee. "I want you and Tex to go with me to Spade. Get the kid away from there and he'll tell a different story. This one sounded like he'd learned it by heart. Helen — Miss Dahl said it was word for word what Don Yoder told her. That didn't ring true to me."

"All right," Euston said. "We'll find out."

"Now wait a minute," Larrabee protested. He looked first at Brant and then at Euston. "There's no reason for you to take Kit from Spade."

Brant spoke slowly. "Any reason why we can't ask to talk to him? — with you and the sheriff present?"

"Well . . ." Larrabee hesitated.

"None," Euston said flatly. "A lawman or a prosecutor has the right to question anyone. We won't ride off with him. Afraid to go out, Jared?"

"No," Larrabee answered. He smiled and dropped into the other chair. "Maybe I'm just too cautious . . . legal mind at work. I'll go with you. In fact, I think it's mandatory I go along."

"Tomorrow, then," Brant said.

Larrabee regretfully shook his head. "I have some pressing business to clean up first. It won't wait. Say three days then I'll be with you."

"But . . ." Brant started to protest.

"It's the best I can do," Larrabee cut in.

"Then that's it," the sheriff said. "But we'd better not wait too long."

"Of course not," Larrabee agreed and arose. "But Kit will be at Spade when we want him. He's safe there." He walked to the door. "Come around tomorrow, Avery. We'll get that store for you. That'll keep you busy until I'm free."

He smiled, waved his hand and closed the door. Brant heard his steps across the porch and then there

110

was silence. Euston stirred behind his desk. "Well, well find out the truth about Kit Thomas, that's certain."

Brant nodded. "Larrabee's all right?"

Euston's head jerked up. "What you mean?"

"Well, he's *for* the folks who elected him . . . maybe something like that?"

Euston sucked at his lip and his eyes clouded. Brant could almost see him throw doubt aside. "He's all right. There ain't been a whisper about him."

Brant said good-night and left. Out on the dark walk, he looked back at the closed door. Euston had given Larrabee a clean bill, but still Brant could not quite forget the sheriff's peculiar expression when Brant had spoken of Lois Carter, or the slight shadow in Euston's eyes before he replied to Brant's question.

CHAPTER
ELEVEN

Brant was surprised the next morning to see Larrabee stroll into the hotel dining room. Larrabee's face lighted when he saw Brant and he came quickly around the tables, pulled out a chair and sat down. "I hate my own cooking. I didn't expect to find you here."

"Where else would a stranger go?" Brant asked mildly.

Larrabee hastily signalled the waitress, gave his order, then leaned back with a long sigh. "I've been thinking about Greg's place."

"Anything wrong?" Brant asked.

Larrabee laughed. "Not a thing. Let's have breakfast and go to my office. We can draw up affidavits and they'll be out of the way. Maybe I can get the court to declare you Greg's legal heir before the day's over. If not, tomorrow. But I know you're anxious to get this part of the business done."

Their breakfasts came. Larrabee showed a friendly interest in Brant's home country, but he never once touched on Brant's personal life, Greg, or asked anything about the family. It was a new side to Larrabee, a pleasant though puzzling one, and Brant began to wonder if, after all, he might have misjudged him.

Larrabee at last suggested that if they were to do anything about the estate, they had best get busy. He led the way to the office and scribbled Brant's statements as to his relationship to Greg. He painstakingly transcribed them in legal form.

At last Larrabee dropped the pen. "Looks right. If you'll sign these, then you won't have to wait around any longer. I'll try to get it through today. Don't be disappointed if we have to wait."

"I won't," Brant said and signed.

Larrabee said he expected clients, so Brant left the office, wandered about the street for a time and then loafed until noon on the hotel porch, feet on the rail, slouched in his chair, hat pulled low over his eyes. He watched the life of Gunsight pass by, judging first this person and then that who caught his passing attention. He felt as though he sat on the side-lines, simply a pilgrim who would not pass this way again, and so must of necessity never know these people.

The thought depressed him and he felt stirrings of hunger. He ate and then found himself staring at the empty day. He went to his room and stretched out on the bed. He assembled what few facts he had, but still could come up with no better conclusions than he had already reached. With one exception . . . Larrabee. Recalling his own reactions, Brant frowned at the ceiling, not liking this uncertainty about the man.

At last his long thoughts and the depressing room became too much for him. He swung his feet over the side of the bed and pulled on his boots. A few moments later, he crossed the hotel lobby and went out into the street, turning to the livery stable. He needed to escape from the room and the town itself. He saddled his horse and rode out of Gunsight, riding aimlessly toward a series of low hills. The motion of the horse, the stir of wind, the immensity of this country helped, and before long he rode erect and alert.

A gentle slope attracted him and he headed his horse toward a copse of trees and bushes at the top of the knoll. He let the horse set its own pace, even to pause now and then to crop at the grass. At last he reached the crest of the hill and dismounted. He ground-tied the horse and pushed curiously ahead through the bushes. Soon he looked down the far slope into the shallow passage between this and the next hill. His eyes lifted toward the open range to his right between the knolls. Beyond the easy roll of the range land, forming a barrier along the horizon, the low mountains made a dark and massive line against the sky.

Brant's head swivelled when he heard a slight sound below in the swale. He instinctively stepped back. The sound was repeated and then a horse and rider appeared around the shoulder of the hill. Brant could not mistake the long coat and dark trousers. The rider halted almost directly below and lifted his head to look along the crest of the hills. Brant stood motionless and Larrabee's swift, searching gaze swept on and beyond him. Satisfied, Larrabee eased into the saddle and waited.

114

Brant frowned, puzzled. Then he caught a slight movement in the opposite direction. Another rider appeared — Lois! The moment she saw Larrabee she waved and smiled Larrabee hastily dismounted and steppped up to her when she reined in her own horse.

The attorney held up his arms and Lois dropped out of the saddle Larrabee swung her around and close into his arms. Her head lifted to meet his long kiss.

The two stepped apart, but still held hands. Larrabee spoke and she replied. Brant could hear only the tones of their voices but could not catch the words. Larrabee gestured holding up a finger as though to drive something home. Lois listened, nodded now and then.

Brant looked impatiently around the screen of bushes the slope just ahead, hoping that he might find some way to get closer. But this was the only cover and he had to stay at this distance, so tantalizingly near and yet . . .

Apparently Lois said something wrong for Larrabee forcefully shook his head and Brant heard the single word "No!" Then Larrabee's tone lowered and he spoke with quicker gestures. Lois frowned, became uncertain and worried. Larrabee continued to speak and then suddenly stopped. He held his arms out, stepped to her. Once more they kissed, then Larrabee stroked her cheek and spoke so low that not even the tone carried to Brant.

He turned to his horse, stepped into the saddle. He looked down at her a moment and then lifted his hand and rode back toward Gunsight Lois Carter wandered aimlessly, her head down in thought.

As Brant watched she abruptly turned to her horse and mounted. She looked in the direction Larrabee had gone then slowly turned her horse about. Even at this distance her expression was a strange mixture of confidence and uncertainty. She disappeared in the direction of Circle C.

Brant mounted his horse and started toward Gunsight. He let the horse move at its own pace, wanting to think this thing out. He wondered just where Larrabee would draw, the line between his duty as prosecutor and his natural inclination to help Carter. Maybe Larrabee took Circle C pay.

Brant came out of the hills. He had ridden slowly to give the lawyer plenty of time to reach town. Brant did not want to come in too soon for fear Larrabee might be suspicious. As he rode toward the stable, he glimpsed the attorney going into his office. Larrabee caught sight of Brant, waved and disappeared.

Brant rode on, lean face impassive. He left the horse at the stable and went to the hotel. Later he went down to the lobby after full dark had fallen and went into the restaurant. There was little in the meal to relieve the boredom. Tomorrow, perhaps, he could ride out to Spade with Euston and Larrabee. After the meal, he wandered along the street, indulging in a cigar, a single drink at the bar and a boring talk about the weather. He walked slowly back to the hotel. The lobby was empty, except for the clerk who nodded to him and continued to stare out on the dark street. Brant mounted the steps and walked down the hall to his room.

116

He started to unlock it when some inner warning struck. He snapped the lock all the way back, then flattened against the wall. He expected the blast of guns but there was only silence. Brant waited then reached cautiously for the knob. He silently turned it and then suddenly thrust open the door, slamming it back into the room.

He braced for the long lances of flame from one or more guns. There was nothing, only silence and darkness. Brant's lips flattened and he glanced down the hall, considering his position. It could be Yoder or any one of his men. The moment he appeared in that doorway, he would be bullet tagged. Brant wanted a look at the intruder, if he could live long enough to get it.

A woman spoke in soft contempt from within the room. "You can come in, Mr. Avery. I'm alone. I have no gun."

Brant stiffened, shocked by surprise. The voice spoke again. "I've been waiting, Mr. Avery. You can understand why I did not light the lamp. Gunsight likes talk. I will try not to hurt you."

Brant flushed. He slowly moved into the doorway, but he held his gun ready. It could still be some sort of a trap A faint light came from the window and he could barely discern the shadowy shape of a woman seated on a straight chair near the washstand. Her voice came out of the dark again. "If you will close the door, I will light the lamp, Mr. Avery."

Brant groped for the door, pushed it shut. He heard the scratch of a match and it flared. The woman stood

117

a moment between him and the lamp. It glowed, brightened. She replaced the chimney and turned to face him.

"Helen. Dahl!" Brant exclaimed.

"I don't think you'll need a gun, Mr. Avery."

He flushed and quickly holstered the Colt. He took off his hat and waited deferentially as she seated herself again.

"I have waited for you a long time, Mr. Avery."

"How did you get here?"

"The back stairs." She looked up at him. "Won't you sit down? You're so tall, I feel as though I'm talking to a giant. It's unfair advantage."

Brant grinned and his face softened, the jaw and cheekbones losing their harsh angularity. He sat down on the edge of the bed. "Is this better, Miss Dahl?"

She nodded and then confidence left her. She looked down at her hands, folded in her lap, and the fingers tightened, relaxed, then interlaced again. She looked up, the sea-green yes troubled and uncertain.

"I had to see you, Mr. Avery. I don't know what my father or — the others would say if they knew I'm here. But I can imagine."

"So can I," Brant said. "You're risking a lot."

"I know Mr. Avery. I've come to persuade you to leave town right away." She saw the slow setting of his jaw and she hurriedly went on, giving him no chance to refuse. "I know you feel you owe something to Greg. But you can't bring him back. I will pay you well for leaving Gunsight."

118

"Why are you so anxious for me to leave? Afraid I might send someone to jail?"

She flushed angrily but her voice was level. "You'll send no one to jail but I am afraid of what you'll do — or make others do. I want no gunfight between you and Don Yoder."

"But . . ." Brant started and she cut in.

"Don acted according to his own lights. I understand how you feel and I also understand why Don hung — a rustler. It's the old law of the range. You are both right in what you believe. Why not let it rest that way?"

"That's the way you think?" Brant asked slowly.

"What else can I think! Beef was stolen. It was found at your brother's place. They had trouble with him and so they only did what a court would have later done. No cattle country jury would let a rustler go free. You know what the penalty is."

Brant's lips flattened. "Miss Dahl, you never knew Greg except here. I've known him all my life. At home he was a big, laughing sort of man, always with great ideas, always excited about something. He was the kind a kid brother like me would worship — and did."

"I — I'm sorry, Mr. Avery."

"So am I. That's the way he was when he drifted away from home. I've never seen him since. He's in Gunsight's boothill and I know nothing will bring him back again."

"Then you will give this up!"

Brant continued as though he hadn't heard. "Then I get word he's hung as a rustler. I knew that was wrong. I come up here to clear his name and prove his killers were liars. I'm beginning to learn that maybe he was exactly what they said he was. Can you know how much that hurts?"

He looked up at her, eyes again hard but faintly misty. Her lips moved in sympathy and her voice was low and gentle. "I think so, Mr. Avery. All the more reason . . ."

His hand made a slashing motion that cut her short. "But Don Yoder did not have the right to hang Greg, to condemn just on suspicion, or to keep him from a fair trial. If a court had proved Don Yoder right, then maybe I could forget it. As it is, Don Yoder murdered my brother."

Helen drew back, shaken. She made a helpless gesture moistened her lips. "Try to understand, Mr. Avery. Don is a high tempered man. He has always been quick to strike back. He does it without thinking."

Brant's eyes locked with hers. "How did Greg injure him?"

"Why — he stole Circle C beef!"

"Set me straight if I'm wrong. Don Yoder is a man who always does the thing that directly benefits him. Sure, he ramrods Circle C and is responsible for the beef. But why should he run the risk of a murder charge by hanging a man? Why wouldn't he bring him into Gunsight and turn him over to Tex Euston? How did Greg's hanging help Don Yoder?

"Some things I can't answer, Miss Dahl, no matter how I turn them around. I've learned that Yoder's riders wanted to bring Greg into Euston. So why did he go ahead with the lynching?"

120

He paced to the door and back. "Why wasn't Greg allowed to talk? Yoder managed to shut him up clean to the time the noose cut off his breath for good. I can't savvy that. Something else . . . if Yoder was right, why is every witness shut up for good, or run out of the country? Why is Kit Thomas kept on Spade and no one can get to him?

". . . I never thought . . ." She started but Brant wheeled to the window and spoke harshly over his shoulder. "Has Don Yoder ever tried to explain this? Or have you asked him?"

He heard a faint stir behind him but Brant did not turn. He heard the door open and he wheeled about. Helen slipped out into the hall. Brant strode across the room but she shook her head, refusing his company.

Immediately after breakfast the next morning, Brant walked into Euston's office. The sheriff still lingered over his last cup of coffee and he waved Brant to a chair. "You look all fired up for action. Me, I can't get to tracking yet. Getting old, I reckon."

"Let's go to Spade," Brant said. He looked impatiently about the big room. "We're letting time get away from us."

"Yeah," Euston sighed and took another long drink. "You got a burr under your saddle. Let's get Larrabee."

Brant walked impatiently beside him down the street to the lawyer's office. When they entered, Larrabee wheeled around from his desk. His eyes lighted when he saw Brant.

"Glad to see you. Greg's place is yours. Here's the papers."

Brant accepted them, feeling at least a bit of progress had been made. Euston told Larrabee they had come for him to ride with them to Spade. Larrabee shook his head.

"I'm tied up with clients and the court until late afternoon."

Brant's face darkened. "They'll get Kit Thomas out of there if we keep on waiting."

"I don't think so." Larrabee made a placating gesture. "But I agree we should get his story. Brant, why don't you go out to Greg's place today? First thing in the morning, Tex and I will meet you there and we'll go to Spade. Greg's place is right up the road."

"I'd like to see Kit today," Brant insisted.

"Be reasonable, Avery. I'm working on your side but I can't let everything else go. First thing in the morning. I promise."

"Sounds reasonable," Tex said to Brant.

Brant's suspicion of Larrabee blazed high again. Still, the man's reason for further delay made sense. He shrugged in resignation. "All right. See you first thing in the morning." He walked to the door, swung around. "If you don't show, I'm going to Spade anyhow."

"Get yourself in trouble?" Euston asked sharply. "You stay at Greg's place. We'll be there."

Brant went to the hotel and checked out, and then rode toward Greg's place. After arriving at his brother's ranch, he drew rein and looked at it. It was his now, all of it. He wondered what he would eventually do with it. This could become a new home up here. He rejected the thought. There was already too much against him if he accomplished his mission.

Brant rode to the stable. He turned the horse into a stall, unsaddled, and looked around. One of the other stalls had been recently used, perhaps as late as last night. Jim Wolf must have slipped back, he thought.

Brant picked up his warbag and rifle, walked toward the house. He crossed the porch and dropped the warbag to reach for the knob. Before he could touch it, the door opened.

Brant stared at a woman with golden blonde hair and blue eyes that boldly met his, slowly deepened. Her red lips broke into a smile and the eyes grew sultry.

"Yeah," she said. "You look like him, all right. I wondered how long I'd have to wait for you."

CHAPTER
TWELVE

Brant stared. She wore a dark dress of cheap material, but even a gunnysack could not have hidden the rich, curving body, the thrust of the breasts, the rounded hips. Her eyes mocked him and she laughed.

"Come in . . . come in! I wouldn't keep a man out of his own house."

Brant caught his voice. "Who are you?"

She touched her golden curls as she studied him. "Belle Rainey. Don't tell me you ain't heard that name!"

Brant tipped his hat back with his thumb. He looked at the corrals, the stable, the silent store, and Belle smiled.

"There ain't no one else. Just me. Come in."

Brant picked up his warbag and stepped inside. Belle walked across the room with an undulating step, sat down in a chair and crossed her legs. Her eyes moved slowly from his head to the dusty tips of his boots.

"Bigger'n Greg, I'd say, even though he always called you the kid brother."

"He spoke of me?" Brant asked. He sat down on the horse-hair sofa, dropped his hat on the floor.

He judged Belle to be about twenty, if that old. She had a figure that would cause any man to look twice, and maybe more, and Belle was obviously aware of it. Her features were pretty, the lips full and moist, the cheeks touched with a healthy outdoors red. Give her five years, Brant judged, and she'd get plump, maybe before then. Belle had but a short time to make use of her assets.

"Greg always mentioned you," she said. She again touched the blonde hair that fell about her shoulders. "Now, I wish you'd showed up earlier."

Brant smiled. He wondered why she had come here, taking a certain amount of risk to see him. He wondered, too, if she told the truth about being alone. Maybe some of Rainey's wild bunch would be lurking outside, ready to appear at a given signal.

Now she was still, eyes sharp and boring. "Did you come to even the score for Greg?"

"Yes." He said no more.

Belle's face lighted. "I knew it! No brother of Greg could be anything but his kind of man. If there'd been just one more even half his size . . ."

"Wasn't there?"

Her lips curled disdainfully. "Oh, Greg figured he had lots of friends. But every one of 'em lost his guts when it counted."

"Jeff Rainey's boys?" Brant asked.

She smiled. "Not them. They just cash in on Jeff's brains. This bunch of greasy sack ranchers, homesteaders and hoemen always hung around Greg and asked his advice. They always egged him on to call taw on the

Association. Greg felt big around them. He was scared of nobody. He wrote letters to the papers and he told the truth about the Association. The newspapers printed 'em, too."

Brant pursed his lips thoughtfully. "I bet that didn't make Carter, Dahl, or any of the others love him."

"They hated him." She sighed. "I believe they hung Greg because of them letters as much as for anything else. He was a leader for everyone who didn't belong to the Association. He told 'em what to do. He talked for 'em."

Brant nodded. "It sounds like Greg."

"I knew once the Association was broken, Greg Avery would be a real important man. I could see that in him."

She fell into a morose silence until Brant asked questions. At first she answered shortly and sullenly, but at last she spoke volubly. She and Greg had been attracted to one another from the first moment they had met at Rainey's camp. Belle told how Greg came riding back several times and how at last, with her brother's consent, he brought her down out of the hills to stay here with him. Greg had lost his head and heart to this woman.

"Crazy jealous over me," Belle said pridefully. "Men had to be careful how they looked at me when Greg was around. Had to watch him real close. He got mad about a gent in town and swore there'd be real trouble if the man fooled around."

"Was there?"

"Came to nothing. Greg never found any proof of anything." She continued talking and Brant realized that Greg was more in love with her than she with him. Belle knew she had a good man, one who would go far. So she stuck with him, pushed him along, openly and subtly. Her honesty was sometimes shocking. She stayed with Greg but she thought it would not be wise to marry him until he had at least come close to the goal she had set for him. Until then, Belle might want to turn to some other man if Greg failed.

This strange mixture of affection and a cold calculation angered Brant, yet he felt a grudging admiration for Belle. She had no education and had undoubtedly lived all her life on the edge of the law. Yet little side expressions or statements revealed a charity and understanding beyond that of most. Then with the next breath she'd seem hardly more than a scheming, pretty tramp.

Brant realized that he judged her by his own standards. Belle Rainey did not know morals existed and Brant might as well expect a cougar to live by the Ten Commandments. Belle could be accepted only on her own terms.

Brant brought the talk to the time of Greg's hanging and Belle's face suffused in anger that gave way to honest tears. She gained control of herself, looked at Brant through misty eyes. "I reckon Greg'll always sort of be with me. Can't get him away . . . reckon I don't want to."

"What happened that day, Belle?"

She thought a second. "I was in the kitchen and I didn't see the Circle C bunch ride up. Greg, Jim and the kid were out at the pens. I come in here to sit down a minute." She pointed through the window. "I saw this bunch of riders and Greg in the middle, mad as hell and arguing. When I saw Don Yoder, I knew something was bad wrong. I couldn't see Jim Wolf, and the kid had skedaddled. I went outside to see what I could do."

She sighed. "I guess you've heard the story, one way or another. Don Yoder had his mind made up to kill Greg. You could tell it. Greg'd try to talk but Don'd out-shout him or slap him with his lariat coil. Once he hit Greg with his fist. I think he tried to make Greg fight back, or break away, so that he would have a good excuse to shoot him."

Brant's face grew bleak. Belle continued. "I come helling out of the house. Yoder grabbed me and threw me at one of his riders. He said I was another damn' rustler and deserved no better than any of 'em. I got real scared then. Remember what they did to Cattle Kate just a year ago?"

Brant nodded and Belle went on. "Yoder said he was hanging Greg. Some of the riders didn't like that a little bit. They wanted to take Greg to Gunsight and turn him over to Tex Euston. Yoder wouldn't even listen. He had worked himself up into a real lather and I wouldn't've been surprised if he hadn't shot one of his own men then and there. They sort of figured that way, too, and they shut up. Yoder yelled that Euston was only a homesteader with a badge and he'd let Greg escape and never come to trial. It was time, the Association taught the greasy sack outfits they couldn't steal beef and get away with it."

Belle shook her head. "I keep seeing Greg. He was in bad trouble and he knew it, but he wouldn't crawl an inch. He cussed Yoder, said he had the right of a trial, dared Yoder to drop his guns and face him bare-fisted like a man. He told Yoder he was no better than a yellow-bellied killer if he turned this into a lynching.

"Then Circle C riders kept trying to talk sense into Yoder. But he ordered 'em to get to the stable and hitch up a buck-board. He sent another into the house for a couple of chairs. That's when I learned I was to hang right beside Greg if Yoder had his way."

"You!"

"Me," she nodded. "Greg was right and Yoder knew it. He didn't want me around as a witness if something ever come up: The men didn't like the idea of hanging a woman at least a pretty one like me. They argued some more and then Yoder got quiet mean. He drew his Colt and said the next'n that argued would get a bullet. He was boss if he had to kill 'em all and then do the hanging himself.

"By then they had the buckboard and the chairs. They tied Greg in one of the chairs. He was still cussing 'em. Between Yoder whipping 'em on and Greg cussing, they finally got mad but they could only take it out on Greg. They shut him up with a gag."

"Yoder should be proud of that day's work!" Brant said harshly.

"Now ain't he!" Belle agreed. "They tied me but one of the riders made the knots so loose they practically dropped off my wrists. This gent got between me and Yoder. He gave me a shove and I got the idea damn' fast. I ran for the brush. I heard Yoder yell and a gun blast a couple of times. Some of those boys got in his way and spoiled his aim. I got in that brush in a hurry and stayed there."

"Did you see Greg — hanged?"

"I saw them take him away. I didn't so much as wiggle in that brush. Yoder would've killed me for sure. When they drove off . . ."

"Greg in the buckboard?" Brant interrupted.

"Tied tight in the chair. I could still hear Yoder cussing until they were out of sight. Yoder led the way with the Circle C men close around the buckboard. That's the last I saw him. The minute they were out of sight, I saddled a horse and headed for the hills. I figured I was dead if Yoder caught sight of me."

"And you stayed there?" Brant asked.

"Where else? I didn't want to get in sight of any Circle C or other Association rider. Then I heard you'd come."

"How?"

"Jim Wolf. Jeff was mighty glad to hear you'd come and he wanted to come down and look you over. But I persuaded him I'd be the one to do that."

"Why?"

"I know men," she answered simply. "What do you intend to do about Greg?"

"I want Yoder hung!"

"I told Jeff it'd be that way," she nodded. "But I had to make sure. You can count on me."

"Thanks. I'll need you."

She smiled and leaned toward him. "Maybe more'n you know. My friends ain't all up in the hills, Brant. I know one gent who's a big man in these parts . . . and he'll be bigger. He wants to pin this on Yoder, too, and he'll do everything he can. He'll be top man in the round-up once you're ready to call it."

"Who?" Brant asked.

She smiled mysteriously. "This ain't the time to tell you. Believe me, he'll do what Belle asks. You've got a real important man behind you, even if you don't know who he is."

Brant realized Belle would as yet reveal no more. Give her time and she might disclose the man's identity. "How about your brother? How were he and Greg hooked up?"

Belle arose and shook her head. "I promised Jeff I wouldn't talk without he says I can. He'll be down when I send word you re like Greg. If he likes you, Jeff'll tell you what the deal was."

Brant would enter no rustling deal, but he must know who was involved with Greg. More important, Jeff's sister and Jim Wolf could easily be key witnesses. It would be wise to give the impression that he'd play out the string with the outlaw.

"I'd like to see Jeff. Maybe something'll come of it."

She stood just behind him. Her voice lowered. "Jeff expects me back, but it ain't too long a ride if you know the canyons. I could be back here by late tonight if you want."

Brant felt his ears go red. "No need to hurry."

She moved to face him, studied him seriously. "Or maybe you won't want me around, seeing as Greg and me was so close."

"Something like that," Brant said, relieved.

She smiled. "Sure. Don't make much sense when you think it out. Greg's gone and no bringing him back. It ain't like you'd be taking me from him."

"I'd feel that way," Brant said uncomfortably.

"You'll get over it and I think I could like you almost as well as Greg." Her voice lifted. "I'd better get along. Jeff'll be waiting."

Brant walked outside with her. She had ground-tied her horse behind the stable. She swung into the saddle without his help and smiled down at him. "I'll get word to my friend, too Me'n Jeff will probably be down. soon. So long."

Brant returned to the house and stowed his gear away in Greg's room. He went through the drawers in the dark bureau but found nothing save Greg's clothing. Brant then slowly moved about the house, over to the store. He found invoices, scribbled notes, old letters, but they told him nothing. There was nothing here, apparently, to Brant's purpose.

By now it was nearly dusk and Brant broke off the search. He took some canned goods from the shelves and carried them to the house. He washed the dust of the months from the pans and dishes and then stoked up the wood stove, cooked his supper. He ate by the window using the day's last light.

After eating and getting the kitchen work done, Brant walked to the barn. His horse greeted him from its stall with a soft whinny and Brant fed and watered it. Light faded fast and it was almost full night by the time he finished. He paused in the doorway. Purple and black shadows were everywhere and the crests of the mountains were softened in the halo of the dying sun. Light glowed through the window in the kitchen. It was quiet and peaceful. No wonder Greg had written home so glowingly.

It was also deadly. Brant grimaced and slowly walked toward the house. The warning came like a chill, a faint stirring in his mind. One moment he was filled with the peace of the twilight and the brilliance of the first star. The next moment he felt the weight of unseen eyes, the impact of hatred.

He stopped, eyes probing the shadows, the dark bulk of the stable, the house, the store, the pattern of the pens. His ears strained into the night. There was nothing, and yet alarm, jangled along every nerve.

He heard it then, a faint rustle. His eyes darted toward the source of the sound. There was another sound near the stable and he thought he saw a flitting shadow appear at the corner and then fade into the wide door. Brant half turned, gun lifting from his holster.

Bushes moved to, his left and he faintly discerned a darker shadow against them. Brant whipped around, thinking to make the shelter of the house.

Something moved near the corrals not ten yards away Brant threw himself flat and a gun blasted a long flame of orange into the night. The bullet whipped close.

CHAPTER
THIRTEEN

Another gun flashed from the bushes just this side of the barn but that bullet went high. The deep dusk and the swift fall of night were kind to Brant. His attackers could distinguish him no better than he could see them. Brant fired at the spot where the gun had flashed in the bushes.

He rolled as the gun from the corral opened up again and a new one started from the comer of the house. Brant heard the bushes thresh and a deep groan that snapped off into silence. Some one moved near the stable and Brant fired again, throwing himself in a wild roll toward the shadows of a stock pen.

Guns lanced from the stable, the house, the corral and yet another opened up from the water trough. Brant gave Yoder grim credit for setting a neat and deadly trap. He crouched in the shadow of the pen, unmoving. The night was quiet again, but Brant knew the men waited for him to make some move. There were six of them, at least, one of them wounded.

He heard a slight move near the house, instantly silenced, then another by the well, a flitting shadow that jumped from it to the high bulk of a wagon. They were closing in, sure that he would lay low.

Brant knew better. He bit at his lower lip as he peered into the night, judging the distances to the house, the well, the stable. His only chance would be a swift and totally unexpected move. He would have to depend upon his own speed and the darkness to get out of this trap. There was only one weak spot in the ring the killers drew about him.

He listened intently. The man behind the wagon moved further to Brant's left, away from the bushes and the stable. The killers near the house must still be there. The most dangerous of them was the man by the corral and Brant heard a slight move over there. He slammed a shot at the sound, heard a surprised curse. Brant was already in motion. He charged the stable, crouching, a flitting, uncertain target.

Guns roared from all directions. Brant did not pause as he fired at the flashes near the stable, his shots searching for the killer over there. The man shouted in alarm.

Brant suddenly cut sharply at a right angle. The bushes loomed close. His maneuver had been so fast and sudden that the others still believed he attacked from the stable. Guns roared and Brant heard the slugs slap into the logs of the building. Then he reached the bushes.

He held his empty gun ready. He might have a chance to reach the bushwhacker if the man was still on his feet. His guess had been correct and his gamble paid off. No one opposed him.

He heard angry shouts behind him. The killers realized they had been neatly worked out of position.

135

Brant came to a thick tangle of bushes, dropped to his hands and knees. He scrambled into the heart of the thicket.

His lungs labored as he hastily ejected the empties from his gun and slipped fresh loads into the chamber. He tried to still his breathing to listen for sounds of pursuit. There were shouts from the yard, and lurid cursing. Then the sounds came closer.

Brant's eyes probed the tangled dark mass of the thicket. He heard the crash of boots close by, repeated on the other side of the thicket. He held his gun, thumb dogged over the hammer, ready to drop it. There were sounds all around him, now, a muttered cursing, then silence. Brant held his breath, lay without moving, eyes darting here and there. He heard a slight shuffle, a low voice.

"Red?" See anything?"

"Nothing. Sure he come this way?"

"Hell, no! He could've gone any direction! I sure don't savvy how he gave us the slip!"

"I thought we had him. We'd better get back."

"Or beat these damn' bushes."

"Forget it. We could get a bullet like Jesse did. Let's git back."

Their steps receded and Brant slowly expelled his breath. The immediate danger was over but that was all he could count on. He remained in the thicket, listening. He heard voices at a far distance and they died out. But he still did not stir. The bushwhackers might wait his. return to the house. Brant holstered his Colt, settled to a more comfortable position. He could

136

also play the waiting game. These must be Association riders. He had heard no voice that he could identify, but he gave odds that Don Yoder led them. He frowned, thinking that it might be Spade men as easily as Circle C.

Brant waited. Greg's place must have been watched for his appearance. Brant had walked blindly into an ambush. He had under-rated his opponents and that could only lead to trouble. This same mistake had killed Greg.

At last Brant moved, crawling carefully out of the thicket, pausing to listen. Then he faded back into the screen of the bushes. He worked his way to the road and turned directly toward the buildings. There was no cover this way but the night. Anyone watching from the windows of the store or house would catch the least movement. A hunted man would not come this way. Brant did. He held his gun ready.

He took care to make no sound. Gradually the store building and the house loomed out of the darkness. Brant moved slowly, tense, but there was no alarm. Finally he reached the very shadow of the house and stood listening. He seemed to be alone in the night. He bent down and, with his free hand, ran his fingers along the ground until they touched a rock. He straightened and probed the darkness again. He threw the rock beyond the house, all of his force behind the cast.

The rock struck a corral post with a dull thud. For a second there was no other sound, then Brant heard a soft step. Then he saw a shadowy movement. Two men moved from the shadow of the far side of the house.

They faded into darkness as they eased out toward the corral. So the killers waited for him — two here, a wounded man somewhere, and three others who might be anywhere.

Shadows shifted again. He heard a hoarse whisper, an equally hoarse reply. Either the two had returned or others had come up, joining the first two. Brant dared not move now. His ruse had disclosed the killers, but it had also alerted them. A door opened and another voice spoke, boldly and arrogantly, and yet low.

"Something up?"

"Heard something by the corral, Don."

"That damn' Avery!"

"Don't know. Red and Jenkins went out to see."

Brant heard Yoder walk out into the yard and he knew that the search would be widened in a matter of minutes. Brant considered, mind racing.

He eased around the corner of the house to the front. He stepped catlike up on the porch, crossed it and eased open the door. He slipped inside and closed the door behind him. This would be the one place they would never expect him.

He crossed the room, having but little time in which to hide himself. When he reached the hall, he heard tortured breathing from the kitchen and knew it must be the wounded man. Brant eased into Greg's bedroom. Just then the back door opened and Brant froze. He heard someone move about, then pull a chair from the table.

"Was it him, Don?" The voice was tight, with pain.

"Nothing," Yoder snapped. "They thought it was."

138

"Oh," the voice said. "How long we have to stay here, Don? This arm is sure giving me hell."

"Quit crying over a scratch!" Yoder ordered viciously.

"It's pretty deep," the man said. "It's bled a lot. Sure throbbing."

"I'll get you patched up!" Yoder said impatiently. "You'll be all right! We got to find Avery."

"Sure, Don. But maybe he's a hell of a way from here by now."

"Those fools!" Yoder grunted. "We had him . . . right in the middle. Then he had to get away and you have to stop a bullet!"

"It was a lucky shot, Don."

"He fired at your gun flash." Yoder paced a moment. "All right, nurse yourself. We'll keep waiting.

There was silence, except for the harsh breathing of the wounded man. Brant looked about the dark room. He saw the outlines of a chair against the tall wardrobe. Brant eased into the chair. The dark minutes passed. He could see the door now and hear every sound from the kitchen. He could look into the dark yard where four men must be searching for him. He grinned.

A quarter of an hour later he heard a step on the small back porch, and instantly Yoder's chair scraped in the kitchen. Brant came to his feet. The door opened and a man reported they had found nothing. Yoder exploded.

"Damn it!" He has to be around! Get out and watch for him."

"All night, Don? We got to be back at Circle C . . ."

"We got time to wait. Keep circling around the yard. No telling where he's hiding."

The door closed and Yoder walked angrily to the chair, dropped into it, muttering. Brant slowly eased back in his own chair, enjoying this. He set himself to wait. So, apparently, had Yoder. Time passed. Twice the wounded man suggested they go home and twice Yoder snapped at him to shut up.

Suddenly the chair in the kitchen jarred and Brant instantly came to his feet. Yoder jerked open the porch door and called loudly to the men. He ignored the wounded man's queries. There were steps on the porch and then in the kitchen. Brant's thumb moved up around the hammer again and he edged toward the wardrobe closet.

Yoder's harsh voice filled the house. "All right. You rattle-brained fools let him get clean away and Jesse picked up a bullet. A hell of a night's work!"

"Wasn't our fault," a man growled.

Yoder cursed him. "We could've shut him up for good but he fooled every damn' one of you."

"Don, maybe we're lucky he got away. You keep pushing your luck . . ."

"Gyp," Yoder said with deadly intensity, "you don't savvy what Avery could do to us. We're the ones who strung up his brother."

"Who spurred us on, Don! We didn't want . . ."

"You didn't want!" Yoder mocked. "No matter what you want, you're in it. Things would've died down but the brother has to come around. He won't drive off so

140

there's only one way we can handle him. You let that chance slip tonight."

"Maybe we're lucky, Don. One more killing . . ."

"You still can't read sign, Gyp. We can't let Avery stir things up about that lynching. We were able to sort of pass it over, what with our friend and the judge. But you're forgetting we're on bail and can be tried for murder. If Brant Avery has his way, that's exactly what he'll do."

"But the Association —"

"Has done all it can. Once we're on trial, we'll be held by a homesteader sheriff, judged by a homesteader jury. Nothing these people would like better, than see us jump at the end of a rope."

There was a long silence. Then a voice asked sullenly, "How about Jess?"

"Help him on his horse. Head for the ranch and patch him up. Jess, I'll tell Carter you got rheumatism."

"You, Don?"

"I want to look around the house. Ride on. I'll catch up."

"This Avery gent . . ."

"He's gone. If you'd had your wits, we'd have him buried out in the brush by now. Git along."

Footsteps shuffled and the door banged several times. Brant took a quick step to the window and peered out. He saw shadowy figures cross the porch, heard Yoder's voice give a final order. A man led up the horses and a few moments later, they rode out of the yard.

Brant left the window and stood just before the open wardrobe door as Yoder came back into the kitchen. He heard the man clump about, muttering angrily. Then a light glowed, faded, glowed again. Yoder had lit a lamp. He was silent a moment and as his steps sounded, the glow became brighter. Brant stepped into the wardrobe, pushing Greg's clothing aside. He pulled the door almost shut, leaving but a crack. He heard Yoder's heavy tread just outside and then the lamp glow was bright as the man came into the bedroom.

Brant drew back, eyes riveted on the crack of light, gun levelled on the door. Yoder moved to the center of the room, halted, then crossed it and the light steadied as he placed it on a washstand. A drawer opened and a shadow fell across the crack for a second. Brant saw a portion of Yoder's back as he bent to the dresser. The man hastily threw things out of the drawer, even the old paper lining. He pulled the drawer completely out, examined it from every side.

Yoder sought something and seemed determined to find it. Brant wondered what could be so important. But whatever he sought, Yoder searched thoroughly. He was a long time at the dresser and by the time he finished, every drawer and all contents were in a heap on the floor.

Yoder turned and Brant saw the dark face, flat and angry in disappointment. Yoder tore the bed apart, even ripping the pillows. He straightened from the useless task and looked around the room.

His eyes fell on the huge wardrobe, looked away. Then he moved out of Brant's sight and made sounds

142

with the china washbasin and bowl, ransacked the stand. Brant waited. Surely the man would soon give up. Yoder's step sounded close and suddenly the wardrobe doors were thrown wide open.

Both men stood immobile. Brant's face had planed into ugly, determined lines. Yoder's was slack, his eyes wide as he stared at his quarry, and then at the heavy Colt held steadily on his stomach.

Brant made a slight movement with the Colt and Yoder stepped back. Brant could clearly see the touch of fear that replaced his surprise. Yoder realized he was at Brant's mercy, alone, and there was nothing to keep Brant from dropping the hammer. He slowly retreated across the room to the edge of the bed. Yoder did not raise his hands but he kept them well away from his gun.

In another moment the fear left Yoder's eyes and they narrowed, watchfully. He waited, calm and nerveless. Brant masked his own thoughts, but he knew that he had caught a tiger. He ordered Yoder to turn around. Brant lifted the gun from Yoder's holster. He stepped back, dropped the weapon on the floor of the wardrobe and closed the door so that Yoder would not have a chance to reach it.

"Sit in the chair," Brant ordered.

Yoder stared insolently at Brant and then I casually sat down. He was coiled like a tight spring, ready to take advantage of the slightest break. Yoder grinned but there was no real humor in the cruel twist of the lips. He threw his hat on the bed as though he visited an acquaintance.

"Looks like you held a hole card, Avery. I'll give you credit for being a heap smarter than my boys."

"Thanks," Brant answered dryly. "Your boys tried."

"They'll do more next time," Yoder said boldly.

"Next time?" Brant echoed. "Think there will be one? Your boys said you push your luck. Might pay you to listen to 'em."

Yoder chuckled. "I've done pretty fair so far, what with one thing and another."

Brant let irritation show momentarily. "Your string has run out."

"Has it now?"

Brant studied his captive. Yoder met his searching look, defiant, assured. Brant spoke softly. "Suppose I had killed your brother and went gunning for you. But you caught me instead. What would you do?"

Yoder's expression did not change and the last shred of fear had left. He hooked one arm over the chair back. Brant gave him grudging respect for nerves that must be made of ice.

"I'd probably kill you," he said.

"Any reason why I shouldn't?"

Yoder cocked his head to one side and then shrugged. "I can think of one damn good reason, Avery. You haven't got the guts."

Yoder's black eyes challenged Brant, though his smile became set, held by sheer determination.

"That's a bad guess, Yoder. You've made a lot of 'em . . . like thinking you could force me to leave Gunsight. But I don't shoot a man down in cold blood. There's a second reason.".

144

"Name it," Yoder said evenly.

"A bullet's too quick. I'd like to see your neck stretching in a noose — put there by the law."

Yoder laughed contemptuously. "That's your mistake, Avery. No judge in Gunsight will ever order an Association man hung."

Brant shrugged. "A judge only passes sentence. A jury decides. You've used spurs on the little ranchers too often and too long, and they'll make up the jury. Think you'd have a chance with them?"

"A good chance." Yoder's lips curled. "You think they don't know what would happen to 'em? Greg Avery figured he could count on 'em. Could he? Have they done half as much as you have?"

Brant granted Yoder this point. They had simply cowered under the shadow of the Association. But they had no leader. Greg was becoming that leader but Yoder had removed him.

Yoder chuckled. "You won't get your hanging in Gunsight." He leaned forward. "Avery, why do you try to buck it! You've been here long enough to know the score. Get out. You can't fight the whole damn' range all alone. And you ain't got friends that'll stick by you . . ."

"Like yours?" Brant asked.

Yoder nodded. "Like mine . . . every Association rancher and all his riders. Men you've never seen, met or heard about. Even the judge is my friend . . ."

"And the prosecutor?" Brant cut in.

"Larrabee?" Yoder's eyes narrowed, flickered, then he shrugged. "All this talk gets us nowhere, right now."

145

"None at all," Brant agreed.

Yoder nodded toward the Colt that menaced him. "What do you figure to do with me?"

"Let me ask the questions," Brant snapped.

"Why, man, don't bother. I hung Greg Avery. The jasper was caught with stolen beef. That can be proved. He might've had his trial, but Greg tried to bust loose. So we hung him. That's unwritten range law since the beginning of time. There's witnesses to prove what Greg did."

"It's a lie and your witnesses will be liars," Brant said flatly. "You know it, or you wouldn't have come gunning for me tonight. There are witnesses who can prove that you deliberately shut Greg up, you and your men hung him out of hand. That's murder, Yoder, plain murder."

Yoder shrugged. "Where are your witnesses? Me and the boys acted legal. We didn't hide what we did. We gave ourselves up to the judge. He set bail and . . ."

"You gave IOU's, each for the other," Brant said scathingly.

Yoder grinned. "Like I said, the judge is mighty reasonable and he knew us all." His voice hardened. "So what can you do? We wait for trial. We ain't running away. You take me in to Euston and he can't do a damn' thing but turn me loose. So where do you go from there?"

Yoder looked up. "Well?"

Brant made a motion with the gun muzzle toward the door. "We'll go to the store. There's more room."

"Room for what?"

146

"This is the second visit you've paid me, Yoder. The first time you had your riders with you. You were mighty free with your fists. This time you made the mistake of sending your boys away."

Yoder looked steadily at him, lips pursed. Then his eyes gleamed. You mean it, by God! That suits me right down to my spurs.

"We'll see how you feel later," Brant said grimly. "Get up."

Yoder arose and, on Brant's order, picked up the lamp. He looked at Brant, still smiling. He honestly anticipated this, Brant saw, sure of his own ability and of his tricks of dirty in-fighting.

Brant glanced toward the door. "Lead the way. I want you in front of me. Don't try anything."

The night was cool and the stars clear. Brant could see the irregular outline of the corrals and pens and, beyond the stable and barn, the dark, silent store building. Their steps sounded loud, though they were actually hardly more than a whisper. The glow of the lamp was steady as Yoder strode toward the store.

"Hey! Don! That you?"

The voice came from one side of the stable. It must be one of the riders who had come back, a new and surprising element added to the game. Yoder was quick to take advantage of it. He threw the lamp far to one side. It arched in a high loop and, instinctively Brant's eyes followed it and then snapped back to Yoder.

He had jumped in the opposite direction, seeking the haven of the darkness. The lamp crashed against a corral post and the man near the stable yelled in alarm.

Brant threw a shot in that direction, knowing the newcomer was armed. He wheeled, about, gun levelled. Yoder might try to rush him in the dark.

A bullet slapped close as a gun exploded near the stable. A second sought him. Brant slammed a shot at the gun flashes and raced toward the house. He had little chance of catching Yoder in the darkness and, with the presence of the rider, none at all of holding him. He reached the porch, dropped behind the partial protection of the steps.

There was a sudden pounding of hoofs and a huge shadow sped across the yard. Brant snapped a shot at it and instantly the man near the stable sought to bracket him. Brant dropped as the bullets slapped into the porch or whined spitefully overhead. He heard Yoder s derisive yell and his shout to the rider to join him.

The man responded with another yell and fired toward the house. Brant returned the fire, trying to seek out Yoder and his companion. Yoder yelled an obscenity. Pounding hoofs faded away.

Brant slowly straightened and looked bleakly into the night. He ejected the empties and reloaded. He listened, heard no further sound. Those two would not return alone since only one of them was armed. But others must be near. Brant grimly turned to the house.

He did not light a lamp. He locked the doors and set himself to wait. Anger rode him, anger at himself. He should have pulled the trigger while he had Yoder under his gun and the score for Greg would have been evened. But as he cursed himself, Brant knew he could never have forced himself to deliberate murder.

148

The dark hours moved along. Brant heard or saw nothing suspicious. The clock of the sky indicated morning would not be far off. Brant sighed in both disappointment and relief. He went back into the house and walked directly to Greg's bedroom.

He sat in the chair and pulled off his boots. He looked out the window on the dark yard, his eyes moving slowly from one uncertain shadow to the other. Satisfied at last, he arose and unbuckled his gunbelt. He hung it over a bed post and then threw himself full length. His hand struck Yoder's hat.

He sailed it into a corner of the room. That was all he had to show for the night and yet . . . He shifted angrily . . . What could he have done with Yoder? He would have felt better had they battled it out with fists. But even then he could not have held the man.

CHAPTER
FOURTEEN

Brant spent a ragged night, constantly between sleep and wakefulness. Yet there had been no alarm when gray dawn seeped into the yard. Brant drifted off for an hour or so of logy sleep, when once again he jerked awake.

He washed, fixed breakfast, first making coffee strong and black. He ate and then went out to the stable. He watched the bushes, the road, suspicious that even yet there might be some ambush, but nothing disturbed the beautiful morning.

He washed the few dishes then went into the bedroom and straightened the tangle Yoder had left. He picked the man's hat up from the floor in the corner, held it a moment, and then dropped it on the bed. Again he wondered what Yoder had sought so urgently. He returned to the living room and tried to sit patiently on the couch.

Suddenly, he heard his name called from the yard. Euston and Larrabee had ridden into the yard. Brant called and walked toward them with long strides.

Euston waved. Larrabee only stared, a touch of surprise in his face, then looked around the yard as though he expected to see something or someone else. He faced Brant, then, smiled widely.

"It's bigger than I thought, Avery. You ought to do well with it."

"If I live long enough," Brant said sourly.

Larrabee's interest quickened. "Something happen?"

"Light and rest your saddles. I've got coffee inside. I'll tell you there."

They sat at the table and listened to his story. Euston looked angry and Larrabee frowned, now and then rubbing his finger along the line of his jaw.

Brant finished and smiled tightly at the attorney. "Maybe the Territory'll get this place after all. I have no heirs."

"It's — incredible," Larrabee said slowly. "They surely won't risk more trouble to shut you up."

"They have," Brant said shortly.

"Of course," Larrabee continued thoughtfully, "you actually have no proof of the assault. I believe you but it would be your word against Yoder's, and the other five. Without supporting evidence, it wouldn't mean much."

"I've got something." Brant left the room, returned and put Yoder's hat on the table. "Our friend left this behind."

He pulled out the sweat band and showed them the crude DY cut into the thin leather. Larrabee and Euston examined it and the sheriff looked questioningly at Brant. "Want me to arrest him?"

"Now wait," Larrabee interposed. "It's not quite enough. Brant could have picked this up somewhere, or stolen it. If I were defending Yoder, I'd certainly throw that suspicion on the court."

Brant nodded. "I won't press charges, Tex. I doubt if Circle C would let Yoder go to jail. Maybe it'd be best to save this for the big trial."

"I don't savvy," Euston said.

Brant tore the hatband out and put it in his pocket. "You can testify where and how I got the band. If we get to trial, we can bring in the way Yoder has tried to shut me up or run me out. The band'll be part of the evidence."

Larrabee leaned back. "I think he's right, Tex. No use trying to jail Yoder for a few months when we can try for a life sentence."

"Or a rope," Brant added.

Larrabee pushed himself to his feet. "We're just talking the future. Let's get to Spade and see what we can do to bring it about."

The three of them went out in the yard. Larrabee and Euston waited while Brant saddled his horse and then they headed for Spade. As they rode, the attorney spoke eagerly and hopefully of the eventual trial. It would make his reputation, would assure him of the voters support for another term. Or maybe, if he handled it right, he could look forward to a more important political office

They rounded a turn and saw Spade buildings ahead. A rider came toward them and Brant recognized Helen Dahl. She pulled to the side of the trail and awaited their approach. Her sea-green eyes looked questioningly at Euston, at Larrabee and then darkened distrustfully as she glanced at Brant

"This is a surprise, Tex. You don't often come to Spade."

"Law business, Helen," he said.

"Law?"

"We want to talk to Kit," Larrabee cut in smoothly.

"But Kit" she started and broke off sharply, still looking at Larrabee Brant threw a swift glance at the attorney but his handsome face disclosed nothing. Helen lifted the reins. "I'll go to the house with you."

"No need," Larrabee said easily.

"I want to."

She swung in beside them, riding near Euston and just ahead of Brant and Larrabee. Brant studied her slender, straight back, caught the bronze sheen of her hair again. He wondered what she had intended to say about Kit, and if Larrabee had silenced her with some hidden sign. They came into the yard and rode directly for the house. As they approached, Dahl came out on the porch.

He looked questioningly at Helen and then at the others. "Howdy, Tex," he said evenly. "What brings you to Spade? and you, Jared?"

"We'd like to talk to Kit," Tex answered.

Dahl's voice held an edge. "Kit? Why?"

Larrabee cut in, swinging out of the saddle. "Why Ed it's just law business. Nothing wrong, is there?"

"There's no use throwing words back and forth. We come to talk to Kit. I reckon we could use authority around, but there'll be no need for it," grunted the sheriff.

Dahl smiled, a cold movement of the lips. "That's right, Tex. I can't let you see Kit. He left Spade last night."

"What!" Brant exploded.

Dahl's glance cut to him and then back to Euston. "Don't know where he went — just slipped off."

Brant's fist pounded the saddle horn. "You've hidden the kid again on some other Association spread!"

"Now, Brant," Larrabee said soothingly.

Helen looked strangely at her father. "Dad why . . ."

"He run off," Dahl said, a touch of anger in his voice. "I don't like being called a liar, Avery."

"No harm meant, Ed," Larrabee pushed in between Brant and the man on the porch. "But we wanted to talk to him . . ."

"Now wait a minute," Tex cut in. "Ed, maybe you'd better tell us more about this. Damn funny he picks just this time to skip out."

"Not so funny," Dahl said coldly. "I always had the boys keep an eye on him. I figured he might take to the hills, even from the start. But the boys didn't watch him close."

"Last night?" Tex asked.

Dahl nodded. "He had supper at the cookshack and afterward he was with the rest of they crew out in the yard. When they turned in, Kit wasn't around. They didn't think much of it for a time but finally they told me about it."

"What did you do?" Brant asked tightly.

154

"Nothing we could do then, Avery. This morning I sent the boys out scouting for him."

"I'll bet they didn't find him," Brant snapped.

Dahl flushed. "I figure he's joined up with the outlaw bunch. You're right, Avery. We might not see him again."

Brant's nostrils pinched with little white anger crescents. "I'm betting Kit has been shut up or hidden, moved off Spade." He leaned forward. "I also bet he'll turn up dead — like Greg."

Helen gasped, stared at her father who looked both angry and worried. He grasped the porch rail and breathed deeply until he could speak. "Avery, don't ride too long around here. I'll tell you this — Kit Thomas was not hurt while he was on Spade. I did not have him taken off the ranch. I'll ride with you to help find him."

Brant shook his head in disgust. "No need. You'd just see that we hunted in all the wrong places."

Larrabee interposed. "You jump far and blind, Brant. You don't know but what Ed's telling the truth."

Brant looked coldly at him. "I don't know that anyone in Gunsight has told me the truth. No one wants a trial, there are no witnesses. I'll look for Kit myself."

He spurred down the Spade road. Maybe it would be best if he turned gun dog. A forty-four slug would atone for Greg as well as a hangnoose. Brant could never depend on the processes of law that the Association warped and rotted.

Then Helen was suddenly beside him, leaning toward him. "Please! I want to talk to you."

"Why?" he asked coldly, not slackening his pace. "You waste your time."

"Please — Brant!"

Brant folded his hands on the saddle horn. "I'll trade you even. I'll answer your questions if you'll answer mine first."

She conseidered a moment and nodded. "That's fair."

"All right. Did Kit run off, or was he taken off?"

Helen looked back toward the house. Her answer was low. "I understand Ray Carter sent for him. He did not run off."

"Do you know why?"

She shook her head. "I really don't. I've thought all along that this whole business was no more than an attack upon us. I've never liked the thing that Don did, but they said it had to be done so we would not be stolen blind. My father believes that, so does Ray Carter."

"Then why is everyone afraid of what I might find?" Brant demanded harshly. "You knew Kit was to be taken away. They didn't dare let his story come to court. That's a strange way to think if your people are right."

"I know," she said in a low voice. "You've made me — think things over. I don't like it."

"I never did," Brant said cuttingly. "Where did they take Kit?"

"After Circle C? I don't know." She looked up quickly, her eyes pleading for him to believe her. "That's the truth. No one told me anything."

156

Brant's voice lost its cutting edge. "Who headed the Circle C?"

She looked away. "Don Yoder."

Brant's voice grew cold again. "Yoder was busy last night." He told her in a dispassionate voice what had happened.

Her chin lifted. "I don't believe it!"

"Recognize this?" Brant took the hatband from his pocket. "Tex and Larrabee can tell you where I got it and where the rest of the hat is."

She stared, up at Brant, her lips parted with shock.

Brant's face grew harder. "He took Kit last night. If the boy was to be taken any distance at all, Yoder didn't do it. He and his boys spent the night trading bullets with me. I can figure only one thing they'd do to Kit."

"You . . . can't!" she whispered.

"Yoder could take the kid nowhere between the time he left here and the time he tried to gun me down. There's only one way Yoder or the rest can be sure the boy won't talk."

"No!"

"They've shut him up the way they shut Greg up."

Her eyes were squeezed shut and she spoke in a ghastly whisper. "I know Kit was taken to Circle C and that was all!"

"Can you be sure?" Brant demanded. "Yoder makes sure his trail is covered. I'm going to prove this one way or the other. Too bad you're mixed up in it. You're too fine a woman."

He touched spurs and raced away, not looking back.

He sped down the Spade road, needing the beat of the wind, the motion of the racing horse.

Then he realized he took his anger out on the horse, that he struck blindly at anything. Reason cooled his brain and he pulled in. The pursuing horseman was beside him, and Euston glared, grizzled brows knotted down.

"I never expected you to go loco, Brant."

Brant nodded soberly. "I never expected to, either. But the way this bunch kicks the law around and then grins like I'm a helpless fool got under my hide." He looked contrite. "I used spurs on Helen Dahl, too."

Euston grunted. "She acted like you'd whipped her."

Brant flushed, then his eyes clouded. "Let's ride to Circle C, Tex. I want to make sure Kit Thomas is there."

"I had the same idea. But you're not going, Brant. You get riled fast and sudden, and you don't get information that way. You go back to Greg's place."

Brant started to protest then realized Euston was right. He looked back down the trail. "Where's Larrabee?"

"He said you're so damn' crazy to hang someone you can't think straight. Ed Dahl's pretty sure of that, too."

"Is he?"

"And with reason enough!" Tex snorted. "Anyhow, Jared's gone direct to Gunsight. He says he'll see you when your head's back on your shoulders and not before."

He started to rein about but Brant checked him. "How do I find Lee Hinson?"

Tex waved toward the distant hills. "About eight miles from the store, above and beyond Spade. But you ain't going to talk to Hinson or anyone else today. I'll see you at the store."

He glared at Brant and rode away. Brant watched him and then he rode slowly to the main road. Maybe Tex was right. He shouldn't talk to anyone today.

He came to Greg's. As he came closer, he saw a dozen saddled horses in the yard. Brant drew rein instantly, hand dropping to his holster. This could be Circle C back in force, intent on ending what had started so badly last night.

A man came out on the porch and Brant recognized Jim Wolf. He felt relieved and also angered that these riders should have so brazenly walked into his house and taken over.

Wolf saw him. "Avery! You got company. We've been waiting for you."

Brant waved an acknowledgement. Jim Wolf had reappeared, a witness whom Brant needed. This time he would not let the man go!

By the time he had dismounted, Jim had gone into the house and come out again. Belle Rainey was with him.

Belle smiled as he came on the porch. "Told you we'd be back, Brant. Jeff's inside."

She turned to lead the way into the house. The room was filled with men, all of them bearing that indefinable but certain mark of the riders of the dim trails. One sat comfortably in a chair near the fireplace, hat pushed back from a red, freckled face.

"Yeah," he said, "Belle's right. You're like Greg. I'm Jeff Rainey."

He extended his hand and his clasp was firm. Brant spoke dryly. "You made yourself at home."

"Always did," Rainey answered readily. "No offense, Avery."

He introduced them, a succession of names like Tex, Bill, Joe, a succession of hard-eyed men. They were a competent crew. Rainey finished the introductions and then nodded toward the door.

"Jim, take the boys to the store. They've had a dry ride and Brant would appreciate their business."

Jim laughed and led the men outside. Belle remained and Jeff waved Brant to another chair, as though the house belonged to him.

"You've had time by now, Avery, to get the tally on Gunsight. Had enough of Association ways? They give a damn for nobody. They grab all they can, steal all they can, and then call everyone else maverickers and outlaws."

"And no one fights 'em," Brant said angrily.

"Except you," Jeff added. "There's one sure way you can even the score for Greg. You can hit the Association where it hurts most — right in the pocketbook."

"Rustling?" Brant asked flatly.

"It worked before, it can work again. We'll have to make a few changes now."

"Such as?"

"We'll have to get along without the Association man who helped us. He worked for one of the big spreads and it was a cinch to pick up beef."

"Cinch enough to get Greg hung," Brant cut in.

Jeff scowled, but had no argument. Belle spoke angrily. "And I want to even that score! It'll happen, too. My friend'll help us and . . ."

"Forget it, Belle," Jeff said wearily. "You've been listening too much to Larrabee's soft talk."

Brant jerked upright. "Larrabee!"

Belle glared at her brother. "He'll do exactly what he says."

"You've seen Larrabee?" Brant insisted.

"Lots of times. He's crazy about me." She smiled and stretched like a pleased cat. "Of course, I never told Greg and there wasn't much Jared and me could do while he was alive. But now things will be different."

"It'll be the same old talk and nothing else," Jeff said. Brant tried to absorb this astounding information. Belle turned impatiently from her brother to Brant.

"Pay no attention. I know what Jared will do if I say the word and if you'n me bring him real evidence. He'll be glad enough to see me."

"Larrabee!" Brant said in a whisper.

Belle did not hear him. "If he could have them Circle C riders hung, it'd make Jared. He could be a real big lawyer that way and maybe a Senator, a governor — something like that." Her eyes grew distant. "He'd marry me then. He would now — he's said so. Except a lawyer in a place like Gunsight don't make no money."

She believed this, Brant could tell it, and Jeff also realized it. He regarded his sister with an admixture of impatience and pity. Brant remembered Larrabee's meeting with Lois Carter. What would Belle think of that? Was Belle first in the man's thoughts as she believed? Lois Carter could give more of the world's goods than Belle ever could. Undoubtedly Larrabee took from both women. He must be the unknown whom Greg had sworn to kill if he ever learned his identity.

How convenient Greg's death had been for Lararabee! It removed a threat to his own life. Belle's flight and disappearance was to Larrabee's advantage, too. Unlikely as Belle and Lois were to meet, the chance was there. When Belle disappeared, Larrabee was free of this problem.

Larrabee may have seen the opportunity that the stolen Circle C cattle gave him. Perhaps he had used Don Yoder as a cat's paw, building up the man's anger against Greg Avery for stealing Circle C beef. It sounded good as far as it went, but it did not go far enough. Yoder wouldn't risk the penalties of a lynching unless there was profit for him.

Jeff Rainey stirred. "This ain't getting us to an understanding, Brant. Want to keep the same deal I had with Greg?"

"I don't know. How did it work?"

"Simple enough." Jeff gestured toward the pens. "They hold a heap of cattle. Greg had a road brand, looks something like a Mexican 'Quien Sabe'. It'll blot any brand registered in these parts."

"That's handy," Brant said dryly.

"It's all we needed. Greg trailed cattle through the hills and sold them in the next county, at the railroad. Few questions asked over there."

"Where do you come in?"

"Men my boys scout around. When we see a good bunch of beef, we chouse 'em here and put the road brand on 'em."

"And then?"

"If there's no hurry, we fatten 'em a few days. If we ain't got time, they're out of these pens by morning. Greg and me split whatever they brought."

"No wonder the Association claimed it was bled white by rustling," Brant said.

Jeff laughed. "One of their own boys let us know where the best beef was grazing, how many riders we could expect. He got his pay from the Association and he took a cut from us. Of course, that's over now and if I ever catch —"

"Who was he, Jeff?"

"The gent who double-crossed us all, Brant. I been hoping that he'd come to the hills. But he sure gives them a wide berth. He don't go anywhere lately but what he's got some of his boys around."

Brant's mind skipped over those who might fit this picture and one man stood out. A dawning knowledge showed in his eyes and Jeff nodded.

"Now you savvy why I want to get this beef business going again. I hope he chases some of his branded stuff into the hills. If I ever got a rifle sight on him . . ."

"You actually mean . . . ?" Brant demanded.

Jeff nodded again. "Don Yoder. He's the one who drew his pay from Circle C and his cut from us for the beef we picked up. I don't savvy why he hung Greg.

You'd figure he'd let Greg slide out of it. Hell, a lot of dinero depended on keeping this set-up going."

Brant and Belle stared at him. The girl leaned forward. "Jeff, you never told me it was him!"

Jeff shrugged. "It was none of your business. The less who knew, the better."

Belle turned slowly to Brant, her lips parted and her eyes large. Her voice was a whisper.

"So that's why he wanted to kill me, too!"

CHAPTER
FIFTEEN

Jeff nodded. "That's something else I hold against him."

Brant recovered his breath. "But Yoder is foreman of Circle C! Why should he steal beef from his own spread?"

"Hell, the answer's easy enough. Yoder figures that someday he'll have the whole world by the tail. But he can't even get started so long as he's a hired hand."

"But Helen Dahl?" Brant burst out.

Jeff laughed harshly. "Think he'd stop anything on account of her! She's just part of his ambition. He figures she'll help him on the way up."

"But he'd be way ahead if he married her! Her father's manager . . ."

"Of Spade, but still a hired hand. Yoder has that all figured out. He has to have a fair-sized spread to get started. He can save money on his pay but not very much."

"So he threw in with you," Brant finished.

"We've cut him in on every deal. It's amounted to plenty. He's salted it away in a bank beyond the mountains — he let that drop one time."

Brant began to see all the ugly picture now. Euston would love to have this information. Then he frowned. What good would it do? He'd have to prove this in court and his hearsay testimony would not be enough. Jeff Rainey would have to be in the witness stand, and the moment Rainey opened his mouth, he would trap himself. Nothing could force Jeff Rainey to talk in a court.

Brant tried to find some way around this. Rainey was out — maybe someone else? Belle? Not likely, for she would be putting her brother in danger. Jim Wolf? Might work — if he wasn't already frightened of shadows.

Rainey pulled himself from the chair. He crossed the room and stood before Brant, spread-legged, looking down at him with a smile that didn't quite touch his eyes.

"Well, Brant, you know how Greg and me worked it. You and me will have to count Yoder out — way out in Boothill, I hope. Will you throw in?"

"I — don't know."

"Why not? It's easy enough."

Brant made a vague gesture. "Maybe, but I want to think it over. Besides, Greg . . ."

"Want to finish that business first?" Rainey asked in an understanding tone. "Hell, Brant, we could do both jobs at the same time."

Brant smiled crookedly. "And me working hand in glove with the sheriff? By the way, he'll be here before long."

166

Rainey was startled and then smiled broadly. His freckles made him look like a small boy caught in a cooky jar. He tipped his hat back with his thumb and chuckled.

"Working right with old Tex! Now that's something I can't do. Maybe you got something — but you can still make up your mind."

"Let me think it over," Brant insisted.

Rainey shrugged. "If Euston's coming, I can't hang around. But I'll come back damn soon."

Brant arose. "Maybe Jim could stick around?"

"And I'll stay," Belle said. She grinned impudently at Brant's startled expression. "Why, man, this has been another home! I know all about cooking and — things. I want to see Larrabee and you can take a message to him. Don Yoder wanted to string me up right beside Greg. I owe him something myself."

"But maybe . . ." Brant started to object.

Belle turned away. "Want to try to drive me off?"

Jeff laughed. "Brant, she's a hellcat. Let her stay."

He walked out with his sister before Brant could make any objections. A little nonplussed, Brant followed them. Jeff called his men and they streamed out of the store, swung into their saddles. Jeff stopped Wolf.

"Hang around with Brant, Jim."

Wolf grinned widely. "Now that's good news. This beats your camp, Jeff, any day."

Jeff swung his horse about and spoke to Brant. "Don't take too long to make up your mind, *amigo.*

Me'n the boys need action — and the dinero. We've laid low since Greg was killed."

Brant nodded and Jeff led his cavalcade out of the yard. They headed directly for the hills and soon were no more than distant specks on the lower slopes. Brant turned. Belle had gone into the house and Jim led his and Brant's horse to the stable. Brant sat on the steps, looking thoughtfully across the yard. He assayed the information about Larrabee and Yoder.

Maybe Belle might be able to prod the attorney on. She might drop hints about Yoder in such a way that her brother would not be involved. But Brant rejected it. There was no way it could be done. Jim Wolf still looked like the best angle.

Jim crossed the yard with a lithe stride surprising in a man of his size. Brant arose and jerked his thumb toward the store. "I reckon we could have a drink?"

Jim's wide grin flashed. "The only time I've ever said 'No' was when they asked if I had enough."

They went to the store. In a few moments they sat at one of the tables in the barroom side and Brant lifted his glass to Jim as he drank. He put the empty glass on the table. "Rainey tells me some mighty surprising things."

"A good man to tie in with, Brant. Greg always figured it that way."

"Sure, while it lasted. Jim, you didn't tell me the whole truth about Yoder."

"That was Jeff's job."

Brant filled Jim's glass again, leaving his own empty. "This thing about Yoder makes everything different. No

168

wonder he sent you out of the country, and I see now why you're afraid to show yourself. Damn it, man! You should tell this to the sheriff! Yoder wouldn't have a chance no matter what the Association tried — and they'd let him hang if they knew."

Jim shook his head. "Now don't start talking like that, Brant. I dasn't open my mouth and you know it. Yoder ain't a man to fool around with."

"And that's exactly what you're doing, Jim."

"Me!" Now listen to reason . . ."

"You listen, Jim. Yoder could take a chance so long as you were shipped off to Idaho. Now you're back. That means you can talk anytime, anywhere. Yoder can't risk that."

"He knows I'll keep quiet," Jim growled.

Brant smiled patiently. "Does he? No, Jim, Yoder can't risk letting you live so long as you can talk. You'll catch a bullet if you keep quiet. You have just two ways of protecting yourself."

"Two?"

"Face Yoder with a gun and beat him. The second way is certain. Talk to Euston and we force a trial right away. Yoder behind bars can't hurt you."

The big man's moon face was serious, uncertain. He rubbed his hand along his jaw then hastily poured another drink and downed it with a single toss. "I never thought of it that way. It's a hell of a risk."

"More risk as it stands," Brant insisted.

"But just me . . ."

Brant cut in. "You and I will ride to Lee Hinton's. He saw part of this. Then we'll all ride into Gunsight

169

and make depositions to Larrabee. Then Euston can arrest Yoder. No bail this time, no chance to get to you. He'll be put away for good."

"Sounds right," Jim said slowly. "But I still don't know."

Brant arose. "Let's see Hinton. We can talk to him."

Jim sighed. "All right. I'll listen and then decide."

Brant sent Jim to the stable to saddle their horses while he went inside to find Belle at work in the kitchen as though she intended to stay here for a long, long time. She looked over her shoulder at Brant and smiled.

"Jim and me will ride to Hinton's," he said. "You'll be alone for a time. Mind?"

"If someone comes, I can head for the bushes. Going into Gunsight?"

"Not this time."

"Wish you would tell Jared I want to see him."

"Time enough for that, Belle. Maybe tonight."

Belle turned to face him. There was something provocative in her eyes and attitude and Brant hastily backed to the door. Belle's smile became wider.

"You look like Greg, but you don't act like him."

Jim came up with the horses and they rode out of the yard and into the hills. They were alert for Spade riders who might chance this far, but they saw no one from the time they left the store until they drew rein in Hinton's yard.

The place was a typical homesteader outfit; a small cabin, a narrow pole corral, a stable, a garden patch. Hinton came to the door, a tall and angular man, face thinned by hard work, dark eyes suspicious, though he spoke to Jim immediately. Jim introduced Brant, and Hinton invited them inside.

He had coffee on the stove and he poured cups around. They talked of the weather and beef prices and then Brant brought the talk around to Greg, the fact that Hinton had reported the hanging.

"Tex tells me you changed your story a little," he said.

"Did I?" Hinton asked, instantly wary.

"First you saw the hanging, then you just found the body," Brant said. "If you actually saw Yoder string my brother up, I want to know it."

"Maybe I got excited at first, Avery. Anyhow, it's none of my business. I leave folks alone, they leave me alone."

"Do they?" Brant asked quietly. "Has Yoder been around since the lynching?"

Hinton made an impatient gesture. "Maybe he was . . ."

"And he said talk was worth your neck. You can walk softly and keep your mouth shut, or you'll look down the business end of a Colt."

Hinton said nothing. Then he dropped his eyes to his hands. Brant sighed. "So he threw the fear of God in you, Lee. How does Yoder know when you'll decide to talk — maybe get drunk and let your tongue wag?"

"Yoder don't have to worry about me!"

"You know it — but does he?" Brant pointed his finger at Hinton as he would a gun. "You could throw him in jail for the rest of his life, at the very least. He won't be safe until you're dead. I'm putting pressure on him. He'll remember and hell come after you."

Hinton looked at Jim, at Brant and then down at the table. His mouth moved uncertainly and then he shook his head. Brant took the granite, pot from the stove, filled the cups again. He spoke calmly. "You're digging your own grave, Lee."

The homesteader's hands knotted into fists.

"You make it damn' black, Avery."

"I just read the way sign points. You'd see it yourself if you'd face up to it."

Hinton slowly nodded. "Maybe — I might be able to tell a little more. But how can I be sure I won't get a slug because of it?"

"You can bank on a slug if you don't talk," Brant said. "All you have to do is tell the sheriff. He'll protect you. Euston will be at my place. Ride over with us. Jim has some things to tell himself."

"Now wait . . ." Jim started, but subsided glumly.

His hesitancy was enough to tip the scales. Hinton shook his head. "I won't ride with you. I've got to think about it."

Further argument would only make the man more determined. Brant sighed, picked up his hat and signalled Jim that they should leave. He said nothing more until they sat their saddles out in the yard, and thanked Hinton for his hospitality and his coffee.

"Lee, I'll hold Euston at my place as long as I can. If you make up your mind, come over and tell your story."

"I don't . . ."

"Lee, no one will know until the day of the trial. By then, there's nothing. Yoder can do. Think it over. I hope to see you this afternoon."

He lifted his hand, wheeled the horse and rode off before Hinton could reply. Neither Brant nor Jim spoke on their way out of the hills. Brant felt defeated even though Hinton had not fully decided. But Brant knew the power of fear that the Association had driven into these people. It was a mighty barrier and Brant could not be sure that Hinton could surmount it.

They came out of the hills and at last the store came in sight. Jim first saw the saddled horse. He slackened his pace. "That'll be Euston. Don't know as he ought to see me right now."

Brant grinned crookedly. "You don't wear an outlaw brand, Jim, at least so far as Tex can prove. He won't take you to jail."

"Maybe not. But I ain't going to talk until I'm ready, Brant."

"That's fair."

Belle came to the door. She was laughing and her eyes danced with deviltry. She called as they dismounted. "We got company. Sure glad you came. How you figure I'd know anything about Jeff Rainey?"

Brant's grin widened and when he stepped into the room he chuckled at Euston's angry glare. "No luck, Tex?"

Euston grunted, disgusted. "To hear her talk, you'd believe she wasn't Jeff Rainey's sister and that he just sits up in them hills to watch the birds fly by."

"There's a lot of birds," Belle said.

"I'll bet!" Euston snapped, then his eyes narrowed when Jim Wolf came in behind Brant. "Now there's another gent who don't know a thing!"

Brant said quietly, "Not right now at least."

Euston drew down his shaggy brows, then dismissed it, glared at Belle. "I'm glad you showed up, Brant. That woman is like a flea on a dog: He scratches where it was, but it ain't. But he's got to keep scratching."

Belle pouted prettily. "A nice thing to say to a lady."

"But a compliment to a flea," Euston snapped. He waved toward the door. "Git out in the kitchen and leave the men to their talk. Makes more sense."

She laughed again and disappeared. Brant closed the door and gave Jim a slight signal. Jim went out to take care of the horses and Brant turned to Euston. "What about Circle C?"

"Nothing," Tex said. "Carter wouldn't say the kid was there or that he wasn't. Wouldn't let me look around none, claiming I had no authority. He was right, since I had no warrant."

"You could get one?"

"Out of an Association judge?" Euston demanded, "against an Association ranch? That's just dreaming. Saw Larrabee and didn't expect to. Said he was there to check on Kit."

"Did he?"

"Said Kit wasn't anywhere around." Euston moved angrily. "Carter acted like a cat that'd just swallowed a bird. Made me mad, but I couldn't do a thing."

"Larrabee wanted to make sure about Kit?" Brant asked, more to himself. He couldn't quite believe this was the reason for Larrabee's visit. He glanced at the closed door that led to the kitchen, thinking of Belle and Lois Carter. He started to speak but suddenly lifted his head, listening. Euston heard it, too, for he glanced toward the window.

"Someone's coming in a hell of a hurry."

Hoof beats sounded with an urgent rhythm that grew steadily louder. Brant and Euston exchanged glances and both arose at the same time. Brant stepped out on the porch, Tex right behind him.

A rider swept into the yard and drew rein with a plunging, dust-swirling halt. It was Helen Dahl. She rushed up the steps, face drawn, angry and worried.

"Helen!" Tex exclaimed.

She had eyes only for Brant. "You were right. Kit never reached Circle C. What have they done with him?"

Brant looked toward the distant and silent hills. His voice was tight, grim.

"Killed him."

CHAPTER
SIXTEEN

Helen stared at Brant, her eyes slowly widening and her lips quivered. Suddenly she buried her face in her hands. Brant did not realize Belle had been standing in the door until she rushed by him and put her arms around Helen's shoulders. She glared at Brant.

"Why don't you slam your fist in her face and have done with it?"

She led the girl inside and Brant followed, Euston trailing him. Neither saw Jim appear in the stable doorway, stare toward the house and then hurry across the yard. Belle placed Helen in a chair in the front room. She glanced at Brant, still angry, and then continued to soothe the girl.

Helen took a deep breath, lifted her head. "I'm all right."

Belle nodded. She turned to Brant. "If they've hurt Kit, I better not wait for you to find Larrabee. I'll do it myself."

"But, Belle . . ."

She cut him short. "Murdering a boy is downright mean, Brant Avery. There's no waiting around to get the one who did it." She flounced to the door. "Jim, you come with me."

"To Gunsight!"

"Where else?" she demanded. "You got a gun and nerve — I hope."

Belle wheeled him toward the door. Brant jumped up and caught them on the porch. He stopped Belle, hand on her shoulder. "What can you do? The sheriff's right here."

"See Jared Larrabee, that's what."

"It'll do no good, Bell."

"I reckon I can judge that. Come on, Jim."

There was no stopping her. Might as well let them go, talk to Larrabee and have their ride for nothing. They'd be back and, in the meantime, out of the way. Brant turned back into the house.

Euston sat on the horsehair sofa, his wrinkled face long. He looked at Brant. "Maybe we jump too fast. It's one thing to believe something and a hell of a lot different to prove it."

Helen whipped about, a new hope in her face. Then her green eyes clouded and she shook her head. "No, Brant is right. I've talked to Dad."

"What did he tell you?" Brant asked.

She shrugged hopelessly. "Carter and he decided it was best for Kit to leave Spade. Carter sent Don over to get him, and Don showed up with five riders."

"And every one of them was at my place," Brant nodded grimly.

"That's why I know you're right. If Don was — attacking you for the length of time you said, then he had no time to deliver Kit to Circle C and still come here. They — did something with him."

Her eyes brimmed and she threw herself down on the arm of the chair and sobbed.

Euston stood up and started to cross to her, his leathery face gentle and distressed. He looked helplessly at Brant and turned to the door, his own eyes misty, one of those men who break up when a woman cries.

Brant felt as helpless. He studied his hands and then crossed to her chair and looked down at her. He had destroyed Yoder — long before a rope or a bullet would destroy his body. He rammed his hands in his pockets. He could have done nothing else. Yet he had not wanted to hurt her.

He tentatively reached toward her, hesitated, then touched her shoulder. She did not look up nor did she shrink away. Her silent crying continued.

He straightened. "I — know how you feel."

Her voice was muffled in her arm. "Do you?"

"Seems like people can be killed twice. Take my brother. He's dead. They said he was a rustler — and then they proved it. It killed the Greg I knew."

"You know that he dealt in stolen beef!" She lifted her head in surprise. "Then, why have you kept on fighting?"

Brant dropped into a chair and tightly clasped his hands. His lips flattened and his eyes grew bleak. "Lynch law and range justice, if you call it that, dealt out with no chance for Greg to make any defense. I don't like it."

He started to say more but decided Helen would learn the whole ugly truth soon enough. His voice lowered, softened. "I found something else in Gunsight, Helen. Maybe the rest of you have grown up with it and it's sort of — the way you live. But your father's ranch,

178

Circle C and all the other Association spreads started here a long time ago. Spade was a little spread fighting for its life, like all the little spreads and homesteads are doing today."

"But what . . ."

"Has it to do with us?" Brant finished sharply. "Everything. Now Spade and the others are big and wealthy. They've banded together and that makes them feel more powerful than ever. So the Association doesn't want anyone to have a chance. None but its own members have a right in the sun. It's not right, Helen, to choke out and drive off men who have a right to settle. Wars have been fought just to make sure of these rights. It's wrong to deny them here in Gunsight."

Helen said slowly, "I never thought of it that way."

"A person thinks like those around him," Brant sighed. "But there it is. If things weren't wrong, there wouldn't be bad feeling about the Association. My brother wouldn't have written articles to the papers or made folks mad. Not that he was altogether right, or men like Jeff Rainey. I hold no brief for rustling and I feel strange turning my back on my brother."

Helen's lips trembled and then her chin lifted. "You think Don's a part of this?"

Brant eyed her levelly. "Don't you?"

She said with a deep sigh, "If you turn from your own people, Brant, where do you go?"

"I wish I had the answer."

She spoke desperately. "Maybe Don has — killed Kit. But I can't believe my father would have any part of it! I just can't."

Brant spoke from his knowledge of Yoder's betrayal. "Maybe he didn't want Kit to talk to me or in a court, but he sure never planned Kit's death."

Helen stared at nothing. Brant watched her, noting the subtle play of expression on the lips, the shadows in the eyes. He suddenly wanted to watch for the rest of his life, a fantastic and futile thought.

Helen stirred. "I — guess I'd better go. My father would not like this, but I had to tell you about Kit. It was important, somehow, that you know right away."

"I understand," Brant said. "I'd feel the same about you."

She looked up, startled, but read nothing in a face that he deliberately kept impassive. Her eyes dropped and she gave him a faint, uncertain smile, and turned wearily to the door.

Tex sat on the porch rail. He did not move as Brant walked Helen to her horse and helped her to mount. His eyes narrowed, lighted, though the mustache hid any expression about his mouth. Brant stood aside and Helen rode toward Spade without a backward glance.

"How's she taking it?" Tex asked when Brant came on the porch.

"Facing it square," Brant looked down the road where the slim figure on the horse rounded the turn and disappeared. "She's one to ride the river with."

"Glad you know that," Tex said dryly. "She always was. Her Dad is a square one, too, even if he does work for Spade."

Brant dismissed a subject that made him uncomfortable. "How about Yoder?"

180

"We'd better talk to him," Tex said. He amended the statement hastily. "Or I will If you're along, there'd be gun-smoke before any of us could open our mouths."

"I want to go with you," Brant said stubbornly.

"Not a chance." Tex looked beyond Brant. "We got more company."

Brant wheeled to see Lee Hinton ride into the yard. Brant immediately strode to Hinton, who abruptly reined in and looked worried to see the sheriff.

"You've come, Lee! You've done the right thing."

Hinton looked toward the lawman. "I ain't so sure, Avery. Right now I don't know but what I'll ride back."

Brant grabbed the man's leg in his earnestness. "Lee, you can't do it! Now's your chance!"

"Something you want to tell me, Lee?" Tex asked as he came up.

Hinton looked at him then at Brant and licked his lips. "I — reckon not. Just come to — see Jim Wolf."

"Hell be back," Brant said and, behind his back, signalled Tex to leave. "Light and rest your saddle. No point in coming over and going right back again."

Hinton sat uncertainly. Tex walked back toward the house. Brant indicated the retreating lawman with a nod of his head.

"Tex won't bother you unless you want to talk. No use riding right back."

"Sure Jim'll be here?" Hinton asked.

"He'll be here, Lee."

Hinton at last swung his leg over the saddle and dismounted. Brant suggested they go to the store for a drink. Hinton looked up at the house where Tex sat on the porch rail and agreed that he could use one.

Brant laughed. "You act like you're fixing for a funeral, Lee!"

"I just could be," Hinton answered gravely.

They walked slowly toward the store, Hinton troubled, giving Brant covert glances but, for the most part, paying unusually close attention to the ground just before his boots.

"Hey! Brant!"

Euston's voice lifted in an urgent shout. Brant and Hinton wheeled about. Euston stood at the edge of the porch now, poised, his attention fixed on the road. A horse had appeared, its rider lying along its neck. The man swayed dangerously to one side, caught himself and painfully pulled himself to a firmer seat.

Brant whirled toward Tex, startled. "That's Jim Wolf!"

He raced toward the rider. Euston gave an amazed oath and jumped off the porch. Hinton stood planted, surprised, frightened. Then he realized the man might need help and he plunged after Brant and the sheriff. The horse turned toward the store hitchrack, moving slowly. Jim Wolf clung to the saddle horn. Brant was still a pace away when the big man let go and tumbled from the saddle.

Brant tried to check his fall, but Jim was too heavy. He slid to the ground, rolled over, face up. The horse shied off, avoiding him. Brant dropped beside Wolf. Jim's moon face was pale and there was a spreading bloodstain over his shirt front. Euston came running up

182

and Brant spoke swiftly over his shoulder as he ripped open the shirt.

"He's been shot. Looks mean."

Brant saw the bullet hole high up in the chest, just below the left shoulder. Hinton came up and stared down at Wolf then, lips tight, bent to help Brant.

"Where's Belle?" Euston asked as they worked.

"Don't know. If we can get Jim to talk . . ." He worked grimly to stop the flow of blood.

Jim's eyes fluttered open. He looked up in a haze of pain and shock and then his eyes focussed on Brant. His lips moved in a gasping whisper. "I — made it. Didn't think I could."

"You'll be all right now, Jim," Brant said with an assurance he didn't feel.

"Bushwhack," Jim whispered. "Belle's dead."

Brant's fingers stopped, frozen. He looked in Jim's feverish eyes. "Who?"

"Two of 'em. Saw one. I got hit, saw Belle go down . . . I reined around — one of 'em — tried to make sure of me — but I rode too fast."

He licked his lips and Brant glanced up at Euston back at the wounded man. "You know him, Jim?"

The man gasped. "I . . . paid 'em back. Sure I got one . . . winged him, anyhow."

"Who was the man, Jim?" Brant insisted.

Jim looked up, fixedly, trying to comprehend the question. Then he tossed his head back and forth, quieted.

"Yoder," he said at last. "Don Yoder."

Hinton made a strangled sound. He came to his feet, stared down at Jim, now unconscious again. Hinton. wheeled about and raced away. Euston looked startled.

"Hinton! Hinton! Come back here!"

The homesteader did not answer. He raced to his horse and jerked the lines free of the rail. He vaulted into the saddle and cruelly set the spurs. The horse lunged forward in a spasmodic burst, then hit its full stride.

Hinton sank the spurs again, and dust boiled up as he headed toward the sanctuary of the hills and his own cabin.

CHAPTER
SEVENTEEN

Brant looked at Tex, face hard and drawn. "There's a buckboard in the stable. Hitch it up. Jim needs a doctor bad. If Belle's dead, she's oh the road to Gunsight. Hurry it, man!"

Euston raced to the stable. Brant worked on Jim, though he did not recover consciousness. Euston drove up with the buckboard in a matter of minutes. Brant and the sheriff carefully placed Jim in the buckboard, then Brant raced to the house. He soon reappeared with blankets, a case of shells shoved hastily in one of his pockets. He covered Jim and turned to Euston.

"Drive slow. We can't take too much jolting and start that wound bleeding again. I'll saddle. and catch up with you."

"What about Belle?"

"I'll ride ahead." His voice lifted impatiently. "Get going, man!"

Euston started the buckboard, moving carefully over the uneven ground until he came to the slightly smoother surface of the dirt road. Brant ran to the stable and saddled his horse. He vaulted into the saddle and sank the spurs hard.

He raced by the buckboard. The road curved, then cut into the hills and Brant was impatient with the impassive, yellow dust, the short stretches that allowed him to see but a short distance ahead.

Then he saw the horse grazing beside the road, reins dangling, saddle empty. Brant pulled in. He might be racing blindly into a gun trap. He rounded the next turn and saw her. He forgot caution.

He jumped out of the saddle and ran to her, knelt down. She lay by the side of the road, face pale beneath the streaks of dirt. One arm was outflung and her skirts were disarrayed, revealing shapely legs almost to the thighs. Brant saw the ugly stain on her shoulder and dress. He ripped it open and expelled his breath in a sigh of relief.

The bullet itself had done no serious damage, other than knocking her out of the saddle. The hole was high, missing vital organs. But she had lost an alarming amount of blood. Brant worked hastily and efficiently, binding the wound in the slender white shoulder, then pacing back and forth impatiently waiting for Tex and the buckboard.

At last the lawman rounded the far curve and Brant waved him on. Tex drew rein, eyes bleak, jaw set angrily. He looked his inquiry at Brant.

"She's lost blood, but she'll make it if we get her to a doctor," Brant said. "Give me a hand."

They placed her beside Jim and then Tex climbed up to the wagon seat. He picked up the reins, glared at Brant.

"This puts us on the warpath for sure."

186

Brant nodded. "I'll look around and catch up with you."

Euston drove carefully toward Gunsight. Brant stood a moment where Belle had fallen and his eyes traveled along both sides of the road. Belle and Jim had been shot from the front which meant the ambushers had been just ahead in the tangle of bushes that came down to the road from either side. Brant pushed his way through the brush. In a few moments he found what he sought. The ground told him that two had waited here. He saw a spot of dried blood. Jim was right on another score.

Don Yoder had headed this bushwhack and the other man was probably one of his riders. Brant cast about for sigh and soon had the picture. This had not been planned Yoder and his companion had obviously been cutting across country from Circle C, making a bee-line for Gunsight. They had evidently seen Belle and Jim Wolf from the crest of a hill and had hurried down to this spot to waylay them.

Brant did not think that Yoder had meant any harm to Belle, but this opportunity to silence Wolf had been too golden to pass. Belle had been accidentally hurt in the ambush, but it still did not excuse Yoder. After the attack, the two men had ridden back the way they came, and they would be almost to Circle C by now.

Brant reluctantly returned to his horse, mounted. He looked longingly toward Circle C, wanting to confront Yoder. But Circle C was far too large for one man to tackle.

He caught up with Euston, told him in brief, clipped words what he had found. He dropped back to look at the wounded man and woman. There seemed to be no change, so Brant came abreast of Euston again.

The sheriff looked around at him. "Don Yoder! The more I think of this, the more I know I got plans for that buckaroo."

"I'll help you," Brant said shortly.

"You — and a heap of others who won't like this story," Euston said.

They said nothing more, each in his own black mood. They finally drove down Gunsight's street. They were seen by many people and questions were called from the plank side walks. Euston did not answer but drove grimly to his house. He gave Brant directions to the doctor's office and Brant spurred ahead.

Dr. Brainerd happened to be alone. Brant briefly told him what had happened, and the doctor grabbed his black bag. He fairly ran for all his paunch, leaving Brant to follow. A group of curious had gathered before the office and Brant tried to push through them. One man blocked his way.

"That was a woman in the wagon," he said as though it was Brant's fault, "and she looked like she was shot."

"She was. Caught in a bushwhack."

"Who!" the man exploded.

"If Tex wants to tell you, he will."

He pushed through the crowd and rode away toward Euston's house, hearing a hoarse voice lift behind him.

"The big feller was Jim Wolf. This is some of that Association's doings hanging, and chasing folks out of their homes, and shooting women."

188

Brant barely heard the growl of assent from the crowd. He dismounted before Euston's small, white cottage. The empty buckboard stood in the street, the patient horses standing hip-shot. Brant ran up the walk and entered the house.

Euston came into the front room at that moment and made a gesture of silence. He closed the door and crossed to the window, staring dourly out on the street. Brant glanced at the closed door, listening, but there was no sound. He came up behind Euston.

"What's happened?"

"Nothing — yet. The doc's working on both of 'em. Says Belle Rainey will be all right, but ain't so sure of Wolf. We'll have to wait."

"The news is over town," Brant said. "Might be bad feeling because a woman was shot."

Euston grunted angrily. "Yoder might as well have set a chunk of dynamite under the range. I've been afraid something'd happen to blow Gunsight apart."

Brant paced to the door, back again. "A range war's no good."

Euston whirled. "When you went after Yoder . . ."

"I ran the risk of starting one," Brant finished for him. "Maybe we'd better get Yoder. I doubt if Circle C will buck the law."

Euston. turned back to the window. "We'll wait."

"For what!" Brant. demanded.

"See if Jim Wolf dies. This could be murder."

Brant paused, impatient, and yet turning this angle over in his mind. A murder charge would put Don Yoder exactly where Brant wanted him. He sat down in one of the comfortable wooden rockers. Euston remained by the window, hands clasped behind his back. At last he sighed and turned, sinking into another of the chairs.

Brant looked toward the closed door. "You'd think the doc would be out by now."

"I put Belle in one room, Wolf in another," Euston said. "The doc's running back and forth and mighty busy. For Yoder's sake, I hope Wolf pulls through."

"For Wolf's sake," Brant said shortly. "Yoder deserves nothing."

Euston looked up at Brant. "You're right about that — but it don't help things. I've been thinking about what you told me." He ran his fingers through his white hair, frowned at the faded carpet. "As soon as Doc gives us definite word, I'm going to pick up a couple of men. I'm going to make you a deputy, Brant. We'll ride out to Circle C. If Yoder's there, we'll arrest him, for murder if it comes to that."

"And if he's not?"

"Well get him. This is one trial Yoder won't get out of."

"Even with an Association judge?" Brant asked skeptically.

"We won't bring him to Gunsight," Euston said flatly. "We'll take him across the mountains and jail him. An Association judge can't reach him so easy over there."

"Makes sense," Brant agreed.

The door suddenly opened and Dr. Brainerd came out. His coat was off and his shirt sleeves were rolled

190

above his elbows. He looked strained and tired. He sat down with a deep sigh.

"The big hombre has a chance of pulling through."

"The girl?" Brant asked.

"She's come around. Lost a lot of blood. It's lucky you found her and even luckier you know how to patch a gunshot wound. Might've died."

Brant sighed. "I'm glad she's all right."

"She'll need rest. Can't move her for a few days. Tex, you got yourself a damn' pretty woman in the house . . . probably start the old biddies talking."

Tex made an impatient gesture. "What about Wolf?"

"He'll make it — I think. Better get someone in to look after him, though." Brainerd frowned. "I reckon you'll be out with a posse."

"You can bet on it," Tex snapped.

Brainerd looked at Brant. "The girl knows you're here and she wants to see you. Don't let her talk too much. That's an order. She's in the room to the left."

Brant walked down the short hall. The doors to both rooms were open and he looked in the one to the right. Jim lay unmoving on the bed, his big face a slate gray. Brant's eyes grew cold and then he turned to the other room.

Belle's golden hair cascaded on the pillow and her face was pale. She smiled weakly at Brant and lifted her hand. Brant held it and pulled a chair close. He noticed the mist of tears in her eyes. His hand tightened on hers.

"Why, Belle! It's all right. You're going to be well."

Her voice was weak. "I know, Brant. Thanks to you."

191

"Now don't you talk," Brant warned. "We know Don Yoder did it. We're going after him."

Her lips quivered. "I — can't understand it! Why did he want to shoot me!"

"Hush, Belle. Yoder thought you were riding to Gunsight to do some talking. He couldn't let you."

She shook her head. "Not Yoder — him!"

Brant frowned. "Him?"

"Jared — Jared Larrabee."

Brant's jaw dropped. Belle moved restlessly. "I saw him back in the trees. I — think Jim's bullet caught him. I — just saw him and then Yoder — shot me."

Brant caught his voice. "You're sure it was Larrabee?"

She nodded, not speaking. Brant shook his head. "I don't savvy everything about this myself."

"Brant, there has to be some good reason."

"It was Yoder who shot you," he said sharply.

"But Jared was backing him. Why, Brant?" Her fingers tightened on his. "Let me know, Brant."

"Well — I think Larrabee has been playing a double game. He's friendly with the Carters, very friendly."

A faint frown touched her forehead. "You — mean — Lois Carter?"

Brant hesitated and then could see no reason for not telling her. If what she said was true, then Larrabee deliberately tried to rid himself of her. There was still another question — what was Larrabee doing with Yoder? Had they been on their way to Gunsight to pull some kind of legal hocus-pocus with the friendly judge? He dismissed that and told Belle about the meeting he had chanced to see.

192

She listened to the end without expression. Then she slowly nodded. "Her, huh? Maybe even all the time while he was fooling around, running a chance of Greg finding out?"

Brant didn't answer. She smiled, a little crooked, then spoke in a matter-of-fact way. "Little Belle up against a deal like that! The Carters could do everything for him. No wonder he didn't try to see me after Greg was killed. It gave him a chance to break off. I reckon he was glad I'd run out."

She wasn't bitter. She accepted the news as she would a statement about the weather. She was obviously realist through and through. She recognized that Larrabee had played her for a fool.

Brant arose and released her hand. "My time's up. You get some rest and don't worry."

She glanced up at him and away. "Sure. I got something to think about now. I can't figure why Jared wanted to kill me, though. Can you?"

Brant shook his head and left the room, glad to get away. Jim Wolf had not moved and Brant returned to the front room.

Brainerd glared at him. "You sure stayed long enough."

"She's all right," Brant reassured him as Brainerd started to the bedroom. "Tex, the man with Yoder was Jared Larrabee."

"What!"

Brant repeated Belle's story. When, he finished, Euston arose, walked to the outer door and Brant followed him. They went to Larrabee's office but it was closed and locked. Euston threw himself against the door. It quivered but. held. Brant applied his weight twice and the door burst open. They need not have bothered. The office was empty.

Euston wasted no time. He led the way to the attorney's house, a place equally as modest as the sheriff's. There was no sign of Larrabee in the house, the small stable and barn in the back, no indication that he had returned and then slipped away again. Brant followed the sheriff back to his office.

Euston gave brief, clipped orders. "Get your horse. I'm getting a few of the boys. Make sure your Colt's working."

In about a quarter of an hour Brant rode out of Gunsight with Euston and three townsmen whom he had sworn in as deputies. Behind them, the town itself seethed as word of the double shooting spread from mouth to mouth. Brant knew that the posse had but little time in which to make the arrests before the range would erupt into open war.

At last they drew rein in sight of the Circle C. A hammer rang on an anvil and a man crossed from bunkhouse to stable and disappeared inside. Euston considered the ranch, frowning.

"Might be they know nothing about this," he said at last, "and again they might play it innocent. We'll ride right up to the house. Brant, you'll go in with me. The rest of you spread out and watch for trouble. If it breaks loose, come barging in."

He loosened the gun in his holster then started his horse, Brant and the other deputies followed. They made a sedate little procession as they came into the yard, rode up to the house. Euston and Brant dismounted. A man stood in the distant bunkhouse door and stared at them curiously.

Carter appeared on the porch. He looked at the deputies at Brant, finally at Euston, a frown growing as his eyes moved from man to man. "What is this, Tex?"

"We'd better talk this over inside, Carter. It's law business."

Carter impatiently gestured toward the door. "All right. But make it short."

Euston and Brant followed him into the house. Lois Carter stood at the far end of the room. Her face was drawn and there were worry shadows in her eyes, though she tried to hold a bored pose. Her eyes sparkled as she looked at Brant and then away.

Carter made no attempt to be a host. "Were inside. Now talk."

Euston held his voice level. "We've come for Don Yoder."

"Then get out. We've been bothered enough by Avery's pipe dreams."

"It's murder — maybe three charges."

"What!" Carter bellowed. Lois clasped her hands, the knuckles white. Euston told him of the attack on Jim Wolf and Belle Rainey.

Carter shook his head. "An outlaw brand, Euston?"

"How about the attack on Avery?" Euston demanded.

"I don't know about that. I sent him to Spade."

"To get Kit Thomas," Brant said evenly, "and he never brought him here, did he?"

Carter frowned. "No, Don said he took the kid somewhere else."

"He did," Brant said, "but I doubt if you'll find him alive."

"Oh, hell!" Carter said furiously, "this is getting too damn' thick! I don't like the idea of a woman getting shot, even if she is Jeff Rainey's sister. Wolf's something else. But this thing about Kit — why in hell should Don do that!"

Brant studied Carter closely. The man was honest in his reaction. "Do you know the whole story of the Greg Avery rustling and hanging?"

"Enough to know that he was guilty as hell."

Brant flushed. "I know that now. But we've found out what Don Yoder's part was in it."

He told the story as he had it from Jeff Rainey. Carter listened m growing horror. He groped for a chair and sank into it. By the time Brant finished, Carter could not mistake the truth.

"It fits. I wondered how that bunch of special beef had been spotted. Don was always a hot-head, but that time he was yelling for blood. He swore he'd get the rustlers." Carter looked up. "Hell, he had to!"

"That's right," Brant said. "He couldn't let Greg Avery talk. He was afraid of Belle, but she slipped to the hills and Yoder didn't dare go after her for fear he'd meet a showdown with Jeff Rainey. He made sure Jim had no chance to talk when you packed him off to Idaho. Kit Thomas was safe on Spade where Yoder could reach him."

"It won't figure any other way," Carter said heavily.

196

"Yoder made you and the Association think all his acts were for your benefit," Brant said. "If you hadn't been so damned afraid of homesteaders, you might have seen through the deal."

Carter grunted. "We were fools."

"You made everything safe for him, buying the judge, making sure witnesses were run off or had the fear of the Association thrown into them. You protected a man who was stealing you blind."

Carter looked at Euston. "Does Helen Dahl know about this?"

"Not in detail, maybe," Brant said. "But she knows."

"A hell of a thing," Carter said. "Don was going there. He come in and said he'd tried to get us a rustler and he had to get on to Spade."

"Will you help us get him?" Brant asked.

Carter looked directly at Brant. "I told you once, Avery, I back my men if they're in the right or think they're doing something for me. I'd have trusted Don Yoder from here to the Pole and back again. Now, I want him jailed. I'll get my guns and have some of the boys ready to ride."

"Just a minute," Euston said. He turned to Lois. "Where is Jared Larrabee?"

The sudden question rocked her. Her face paled. "I — I don't know. What has this to do with Don?"

"He was with Yoder when Jim Wolf and Belle Rainey were shot. The woman saw him. She says he tried to kill her."

"That's ridiculous! Why should he?"

Euston hesitated, then his jaw hardened. "You won't like this Lois. Jared saw a heap of Belle Rainey, even when Greg was alive. She thought Jared would marry her. She was on her way to see him when they were ambushed. Both Yoder and Jared had good reason to kill her."

Father and daughter turned pale. Lois swayed, caught herself. Euston's voice lowered. "I know he was wounded I figure he'd come here with Yoder. I hope I don't have to search the house."

A door across the room opened and Brant turned, froze. Jared Larrabee stood framed, a Colt in his hand that moved from one to the other. Jared's handsome face was pale and Brant saw the bulge of a bandage under his shirt. His eyes cut from Euston to Brant, to — Carter, rested apologetically on Lois for a moment, and then cut back to Brant.

"I've been listening," he said.

Brant eyed the gun. "You're going to use that on us as well as Belle?"

Larrabee's lips twisted anrily. "I didn't shoot Belle. Yoder did . . . claimed it was an accident. Now I know better. His coat was off and his shirt sleeves were rolled above his I've heard everything you've said."

"Better drop the gun, Jared," Tex said sharply.

Larrabee grimaced. "Not yet, Tex. Not until I've found Don Yoder. Then you can have the gun — and me." He swayed, caught himself.

"You'll not make it," Brant said. Lois made a strange, throaty sound and took a step toward the attorney.

Larrabee's voice slashed at her. "Stay back, Lois. You want no part of me now." He faced Brant again. "I'll stay on my feet until I find Yoder. He's played me for the worst sucker in the Territory, protecting him, thinking I could keep him quiet. He knew about Belle and he let me know it. I either backed him all the way or he would tell the Carters. I'd been a fool, but I couldn't let Lois know it. I thought with Belle gone, I could wipe out all the past — except Don."

He took a deep breath. "I didn't like what he did, but Greg *was* a rustler. If Wolf was chased out of the country, that was one less shady character in Gunsight. To protect the Association, I worked with the judge — with Carter and Dahl. I didn't know Yoder was as bad an outlaw as Rainey — worse, he's a killer."

He stepped into the room. "I have my own score to settle with Don Yoder. "No one's taking him until I've had a . . ."

His face suddenly, whitened and his eyes glazed. He fell, face-forward, in a faint.

CHAPTER
EIGHTEEN

Brant jumped to catch him as the gun thudded to the floor. Lois screamed and Euston scooped up the gun. Brant and Carter carried Larrabee to the couch and stretched him out on it while Lois ran down the hall, returning soon with a basin of water and a cloth. She bathed his face until Larrabee's eyes slowly opened. Then she thrust herself back beyond Carter and Brant and stood stiff and silent.

"I — I didn't shoot Belle, didn't even fire at her." He breathed deeply. "I'd come here to find Yoder and see what I could do to protect him from any charges Brant might bring."

He started to sit up but Carter pushed him down. "Take it easy, man."

Larrabee looked toward the window. "We took a short cut over the hills and we saw the two riders. I recognized Jim Wolf. Yoder became excited and said that he had direct proof Wolf was working for Rainey. If we could take him in, it'd make Yoder look better."

"And the girl?" Brant asked.

Larrabee made a wry face. "At that distance I didn't know who she was. Yoder said we could set an easy trap, bring Wolf in. He said we could finish another job while we were at it. I didn't get that at first. We hid in the brush and I was concentrating on Wolf. I figured we'd step out, guns on him, and that would be it. Yoder was a few yards from me."

"Yoder fired first?" Tex demanded.

"He did all the firing," Larrabee said bitterly. "First I knew, he was shooting. I was so surprised I just stood there. I recognized Belle and the next thing I knew, I saw her fall. Then Wolf started throwing lead, and one got me."

He winced. "I pulled myself off but the shooting continued. Yoder came back and said Wolf was done and he'd get me to Circle C. I asked him about Belle and he said she wasn't around. A hell of a way to say he believed he'd killed her!"

He was silent for a long time. "A man can do some foolish things. I'm one of the worst. I got tangled up with Belle Rainey. It didn't mean anything but it was hard to get out of. Then there was Yoder. He let me know that if I didn't cover him every way possible, he'd tell the Carters about my owlhoot girl, as he called her."

Larrabee sighed again. "When she disappeared after Greg was hung, I thought it was over at last." He looked up at Brant, frowning. "I can't understand why Yoder shot her."

"Because she could get him in hot water pronto," Brant snapped. "He had to shut her and Wolf up."

Brant arose and signalled to Tex. Lois remained fixed and frozen across the room and Brant felt a deep pity for her.

Brant put her out of his mind. "We'd better get to Spade Yoder can travel fast and far. No telling now what he'll do."

Tex nodded. Carter stood up and looked at Brant. "You're right. Wait'll I get my gun, and the boys. What'll we do with him?" He pointed to Larrabee.

"Your daughter can take care of him," Brant suggested.

"No!" Lois' voice was strident. Her shoulders were back, but behind the dry eyes and frozen face anguish stirred. Brant crossed to her, took her hand, though she tried to pull away.

"Let's talk on the porch," he said gently.

"Nothing to say." Her voice sounded dead.

"Let's try," Brant insisted, holding her hand. She did not try to pull away nor, on the other hand, would she look at Larrabee. Out on the porch, Brant dropped her hand and went to the rail.

"Have your say," she spoke. "Nothing matters, I guess."

"That's where you're wrong," Brant said. "If you had made a horrible mistake, do you think it fair if everyone condemns you and won't ever let you forget it?"

Her eyes flicked to him, away. "What has that to do . . ."

"Everything," Brant said curtly. His voice gentled again. "All of us make mistakes — you, me, your father, Larrabee. The thing is that your father and Larrabee both know it now, and they're willing to make up for it. Jared's mistakes caused a lot of harm, but your father's and the Association's were even worse in protecting Yoder. Now that's over and I reckon folks will understand and try to forget it. Why can't you . . ."

202

Carter came out, hesitated, and Brant realized the man had been listening. He looked at his daughter.

"He's right, Lois. The worst mistake I made was trying to be smart when I knew you and Jared were in love. I told Jared if he'd work secretly for us, the Association would push him right up the ladder."

He made a wry and self-daming grimace. "I sure put a wrong twist in a young man's life! I didn't see it'd make him think crooked in everything he did. I've come damn close to ruining your life. Get in there, Lois and take care of him."

"But . . ."

"Just watch him, then. But do some thinking. If your dad hadn't been so damned smart, Belle wouldn't have had a chance. You two would have been married long ago." He jerked his thumb at Brant while his eyes held Lois. "He's right. Think over what we've said before you make another bad mistake."

Carter called two Circle C men and told them the news. The stunned surprise on their faces was soon replaced by anger. They raced to the bunkhouse. Soon Carter, his men, and the sheriff's posse raced out of the yard and headed directly for Spade.

Carter rode between Brant and Euston and he spoke in a bitter tone. "I've sure tangled things up all the way around, using those two kids was a nice, bright thing to do."

"It's over," Brant said.

"You hope!" Carter snapped and his voice grew plaintive. "So do I. When Lois first told me, I was pleased. Then I thought that Larrabee would help us while he seemed to be working for the homesteaders."

"That's an old story," Brant said.

"But a nasty one. When Larrabee told Lois you and Tex wanted to get Kit's story, I sent word to Spade that Don would pick him up and bring him here. I'd ship him on to Triangle Bar.

"Don came back with a wounded rider the other night. Said he'd met up with you and there'd been some trouble. Larrabee must have told him where you were. Yoder said he'd sent Kit on, and I thought he meant Triangle Bar. Then Larrabee came this morning, saying you'd been to Spade. Yoder told Jared they'd better head into Gunsight to see the judge because of that brush he had with you."

Brant smiled. "It was a bushwhack." He told then of the attack and of Yoder's escape.

Carter shook his head. "I reckon you're right about Kit." His big fist hit the saddlehorn. "But why'd Don do this!"

"Because Jeff Rainey run a bunch of special beef to Greg without saying anything to Yoder. Then when one of your riders found them in Greg's pens, the whole thing threatened to come to life. Yoder had to kill fast to protect himself — and lately he's had to move faster to cover the whole rustling deal."

"That's what I can't savvy," Carter said. "I paid him well."

"You don't ever pay an ambitious man well," Brant answered. "Yoder had big ideas and needed big money. Even if he married Helen Dahl and inherited her

204

father's job, he'd still be a hired hand. You couldn't pay him that much — a ranch of his own, a chance at wealth and power."

"And your brother?"

"Belle said Greg figured the homesteaders would elect him to an important job. He also wanted wealth. It's all I can see, and Greg sure won't ever tell me."

Carter threw him a flashing glance. "You've had some jolts yourself, friend."

The rest of the way to Spade, they rode in comparative silence. At last they approached the ranch and Tex lifted his hand as he drew rein. The rest gathered around him, all of them looking ahead at the jumble of buildings. Euston sent his deputies and the Circle C riders on a wide circle about the ranch. If Yoder was here and made a break, Tex wanted to make sure he'd run up against a deputy gun.

The sheriff looked at Brant, then at Carter. "You stay here Carter, and watch he don't come helling this way. Brant, you'n me will go in after him."

"Now wait," Carter cut in. "Yoder won't spook if he sees me first. I'll keep his attention while you slip in the back way."

Brant shook his head. "Yoder might figure you'd make that kind of play. He won't wait a minute to kill if he thinks the game is up."

Carter shook his head stubbornly. "I sure as hell started this, the way I've acted. The least I can do is help end it. Sit a while and then move in."

Before Brant or Euston could stop him, Carter spurred into the yard. He rode openly toward the house. Brant reined his horse to the left.

"I'll work to the house from the back," he told Euston, who nodded and continued to watch the front.

Each minute dragged out to an eternity as Brant worked his way toward the back door, after having dismounted and left his horse beyond the stable. Yoder could even now be watching from a kitchen window, biding his time until Brant walked in against a ready gun. If Helen and her father were there, what would happen when the fireworks started? A bullet has no selectivity and could kill Helen as well as Yoder.

He reached a small smokehouse within a few yards of the back door. He paused, searching, ears straining for any sound that would indicate the posse had closed in. He heard or saw nothing. He drew his gun and whipped around the corner of the shack, ran at a crouch across the open space, and flattened himself against the wall beside the door. There had been no alarm, nothing broke the silence.

Brant slowly turned the door knob, holding his breath. The door swung silently open under his slow, steady pressure He looked in upon a huge, empty kitchen. He heard the sound of voices from the front of the house, angry voices — one of them Helen's. Brant eased inside.

Across the room an open doorway led to another room. Brant cat-footed across the kitchen, gun levelled. He looked in on the heavy, long table and dark chairs of the dining room. The voices came from beyond the door on the far side of the room. Brant could see a portion of the front room, the edge of the outer door, a strip of flowered wallpaper. He could not see the occupants but their voices were now clear.

Helen's was biting and scathing. "— your foreman has proved himself quite a man!"

"Now wait a minute, Helen!" Yoder's harsh voice cut in but she would not be stopped.

"He has committed murder — hung Greg Avery to save his own worthless life, killed Kit Thomas."

Yoder yelled, "You can only drive a man so far . . ."

"Man! You?" Brant could hear the whiplash of her scorn. "Carter made you foreman, every other rancher trusted you. I swore by you. You used us all — everyone and everything. No wonder you're afraid of Brant Avery! Well, it's too late. The truth is out."

Brant eased into the dining room. Yoder would not take much of this. Euston and the deputies should be close. If Carter could keep Yoder's attention just a few more minutes — Brant took a couple of step toward the far door and then Carter snapped an order.

"Stand hitched, Yoder. It's the end of your rope. I've been deputized . . ."

Helen's scream cut him short. Brant stood frozen a second and in that time Yoder whipped into the room. He held Helen as a shield against Carter's gun and tried to draw his own. Helen partially blocked it. Brant heard Dahl's alarmed yell.

"Don't shoot, Ray! You'll kill Helen!"

Brant called, "Drop the gun, Yoder!"

Yoder whipped Helen and himself, around. At the same instant he freed his own gun. Brant saw its black muzzle under Helen's arm and it belched flame. The bullet smashed into Brant's shoulder with the driving force of a steel ram. He fell back and down.

Carter charged from the other room. Yoder whipped Helen about and slammed her into Carter, both of them stumbling and going down. Carter tried desperately to free himself of the girl and line his gun.

Yoder lunged across the room, seeking escape beyond Brant through the kitchen and into the yard. Brant dizzily tried to bring up his gun. Yoder's boot connected with the weapon, sending it spinning out of Brant's hand Brant fought off the helplesness that seized him. He grabbed the black boots before his eyes.

Yoder sprawled face-forward, half in the room, half out. He kicked viciously and Brant could no longer hold on. He slid down a black vortex and fought against it. Yoder twisted around and Brant saw the gun come up, but the black muzzle aimed toward the far door. Thunder roared in Brant's ears and flame lanced and laced before his eyes. Then sound and sight faded into a pinpoint of bright light, and that snapped out into total darkness.

He lived in darkness, warm and soft, and yet he dimly sensed the need to pull himself up and out of it. The urge was a point of irritation that grew and grew until it was an overwhelming torture. He moved, tossed, clawed and still the irritation grew. Then the darkness lessened and there was a strange source of light, an indefinable gray that grew more intense.

He looked down an expanse of white to the brass foot of a bed. Beyond it stood a woman and her face swam into focus — Helen Dahl. A man stood beside her, her father, and Brant frowned, puzzled. Just then Helen turned and looked at him.

Her eyes widened and she grabbed her, father's arm. "He's come around!"

Brant realized that he could not stay here when there was so much to be done. He made a move to lift himself. Instantly Helen was around the bed and her hands gently forced him back.

"Lie still. You must."

He didn't have the will to argue. He looked up at her, puzzled, then alarmed. "Yoder! He'll get away!"

A shadow came in her eyes, passed as she smiled wanly, smoothed the covers over his chest. "He's — dead. Ray Carter's bullet caught him — after you tripped him. He died two days ago."

But it was just a moment ago that . . . He shook his head. "How long have I been here? Where am I?"

"There days, Brant. This is Spade."

Carter and Dr. Brainerd came to the bed and Helen stepped back. She looked at Brant, searching and probing, then turned away. Brant's attention centered on the doctor. Carter waited, standing just beyond him.

Brainerd straightened, relieved. "He'll make it. Just a matter of rest now."

Carter asked. "Can I talk to him?"

"Don't see why not. Don't talk too long, though."

He snapped shut his black bag, grinned at Brant and bustled from the room. Carter pulled up a chair and sat down beside the bed. He looked thoughtfully at Brant and then smiled.

"I reckon I'd better thank you, Avery. You run a hell of a risk, but you saved Helen. Yoder nearly got away."

"What happened?"

"Yoder saw that he'd overplayed his hand when he ambushed Wolf and the Rainey woman. He came here with some sort of a story to persuade Helen to leave with him. She let him have it with both barrels, saying he was a killer and a traitor. It was the first time Yoder knew she had the greater part of the truth."

He sighed in relief. "I come in about then. Helen was so mad she didn't see Yoder was on the edge of killing, and I didn't do any good by walking in. Anyhow, she branded him all over again. I tried to take Yoder myself before he could make a break. I messed things up and Yoder would have got away, but you took a hand. How you hung onto him with a bullet-smashed shoulder, I don't know. It stopped him long enough for Tex to barge in. Yoder went down fighting but one of my bullets was lucky enough to get him.

"He talked before he died?" Brant asked.

"Had two days of dying." Carter made a grimace. "Anyhow, we got the whole dirty picture. He'd killed Kit Thomas, all right. Picked him up at Spade and then sent his riders on to your place. Yoder shot the kid and rolled the body in a shallow cave, rocked up the front. Then he came to your place."

Brant remembered. "Jim? — and Belle?"

"They'll be up and around soon," Carter assured him.

"Larrabee?"

Carter booked guilty. "Jared and Lois have made up, and I'm thankful to you for saying what you did. He's resigned as prosecutor. I've sent word to the Association that I've had a bellyful of double-dealing and riding rough shod over everyone. We act fairly and squarely or I pull out. You made me see that, too."

He sighed contentedly. "Lois and Jared are together again. Yoder's gone. Oh, Tex talked to Belle. When she can travel, shell tell Jeff he has a month to get out of the country or Tex will go up in the hills after him. The homesteaders and the Association will make up the posse. Proves we can work together. Belle says Jeff Rainey will leave. So rustling's over in Gunsight."

Brant smiled, content. Then a new thought struck him. "Helen?"

Carter shrugged. "This has been as hard on her as on any of us. She thought a heap of Don Yoder, A girl like that don't just throw herself away. I can guess what all this has done to her."

"I wish it hadn't happened," Brant said.

"Now there you're wrong, Brant. Yoder would have cracked up one way or another. If Helen was married to him, it'd be worse than now. She's a sensible girl, Brant, lots of woman there. She'll get her balance. Someday the right man will come along. She'll be all right."

Brant felt better. He hadn't completely destroyed everything for Helen, after all. He felt drowzy again. Carter's voice cut into his thoughts.

"Brant, what you aim to do now?"

"I don't know. I could sell Greg's place and go back to the ranch where I used to work. Sort of have to think it over."

"Wish you would," Carter said. "I don't have a foreman now and I need one. You'd do a good job. You could keep Greg's place and maybe Jim Wolf could run it for you." He grinned. "But you don't deal in cattle, savvy!"

Brant stared. "Me — work for you!"

"Why not? Tex Euston swears you're a man to ride the river with. I've seen you in action, though I figured you were a heap of trouble once." Carter nodded toward the door. "Now Helen — she says the Association spreads can't ever get enough men like you."

"She says it!"

"Says the little ranchers know you and can trust you. That way all of us can work closer. Maybe there's something else in her mind, but . . ." Carter hastily arose. "Now don't you decide this minute. You're going to be here a spell, under Helen's care. You just think it over. Doc Brainerd'll bust me wide open if I keep on talking!"

He left the room, closing the door gently behind him. Brant sank deeper in the bed. His shoulder was painful and yet he was content. He thought of Carter's offer.

"Why not?" he asked aloud. His job in Gunsight was over for Yoder had paid for Greg's death. He had thought of himself as a lonely, unwanted stranger on this range, never to have a part in its life. Now Carter offered something that could give him roots here besides a chance that seldom came the way of a puncher.

Greg's store and land would in time become more valuable. Even if he let Wolf manage it, he could always think of it as an eventual home. What had Carter said? . . . Someday Helen would find the right man?

His mind seized upon the thought. He felt increasingly drowzy and with it came hopeful dreams. Maybe he could become that right man. His mind drifted on, lazily. Brant Avery, foreman of the Circle C. Brant Avery; store owner, land owner. A good job — fine country and — someday — Helen.

He sank into a deep and contented sleep.